SECRETS AND LIES BOOK CLUB WIVES

When Truth is stranger than Fiction!

First Published in 2021 Copyright © 2021 S J Carmine. All rights reserved. This is a work of fiction. Names, characters, places, and incidents are products of the author's imagination or are used fictitiously and should not be construed as real. Any resemblance to actual events, locales, organizations or persons, living or dead, is entirely coincidental. No part of this book may be used or reproduced in any manner whatsoever without written permission, except in the case of brief quotations embodied in critical articles and reviews. For more information e-mail all enquiries to reallyreallynovel@gmail.com

BOOK CLUB DAY

It's been nearly a year since we moved to this God forsaken village. I don't quite know how to describe it but it feels like a cross between the films Village of the Damned and Hot Fuzz. Everyone knows everyone and nothing is fucking private. Seriously, if you fart too loudly the Chairwoman of the local Women's Circle will know about it within minutes. On the day we arrived there was a procession of ladies knocking on our door. Some had cake, some had flowers and one lady made us a casserole which was lovely and welcoming... but how the fuck did they know we were moving in and how did they know our names? I suppose you are wondering what the hell am I doing here? My husband got a fantastic promotion at work and we thought the time was right to leave the northern city we lived in and move to the southern countryside where the air was cleaner and the environment better. We thought it would be a safer place in which to bring up our children. It may be quieter and cleaner than living in a city but when we first arrived, they were bored shitless...I was really concerned that we had done completely the wrong thing and they would hate me forever. Once they settled into school they thankfully started to make some friends which was one less thing for me to worry about.

After being here a few months and starting to feel bored myself. I decided I really needed to get involved with the local community. I needed to get some hobbies. I found a few options: Horse riding...I can't ride a fucking bike, so that was never going to happen and don't tell the 'ladies' but horses scare me....they're so big and those teeth! Flower arranging for the local church...I lack colour co-ordination and have the artistic ability of a two year old, so again not really right for me. Then there was the book club...now that could be something that might work. I immediately researched ladies book clubs and they sounded right up my street. From what I could gather, you met once a month to discuss a book chosen by one of the other club members and they involved not much chat about books and plenty of eating cake and drinking Prosecco...I thought I had found my spiritual home. Feeling quite excited I rolled up at 6pm on a Thursday evening, bottle of Prosecco in hand and ready for a good old gossip. I flung the door open waving my bottle as if I was entering a house party in full swing;

'Evening ladies, get the glasses out.'

I was met by silence, stone dead silence...fuck me it was awkward and if looks could kill, I would have died many times over. The ladies were sitting in a circle, there was no table groaning under the weight of snacks and alcohol. There didn't appear to be any chit chat and the atmosphere was as far from jovial as you could get.

Nobody cracked a smile and they didn't take their eyes off me. I started to get that 'Village of the Damned' vibe again. I decided to leg it before their eyes started to glow. As I turned to leave, Annabelle group leader and clearly the alpha female spoke and it was as if I was no longer important to the rest of the group as all eyes were on her. They were hanging off her every word.

'Hello Julia, how good of you to join us. Please leave your bottle at the door and take a seat.'

I did as I was told and put the bottle down. I found an empty seat and sat down like a naughty schoolgirl. I'm sure I saw a couple of the other ladies sniggering. Annabelle had a booming voice and she spoke the Queen's English perfectly. I suddenly felt like a northern imposter with my flat vowel sounds trying to infiltrate their comfortable world of Received Pronunciation and Pimms on the lawn. Nobody had said anything, but from them moment I arrived in the village I could feel people cringe when they heard me speak…well tough shit. I'm not changing my accent for anybody…for fucks sake, it's glass not glaaaarse. I kept my eyes firmly focused on the floor. I didn't want to attract any more attention to myself than I already had. The other ladies were probably relieved that it was me and not them who had incurred the wrath of the mighty Annabelle. At that moment, I knew I had made a mistake joining the club and I should have given it a miss. Instead of doing the sensible thing and not going back, I decided wrongly to give it a chance. It was becoming harder and harder for me to drag myself to meetings. Instead of being the highlight of my month it had become the day I dreaded the most. The books that were chosen for us to read were so heavy going. I wasn't studying English Literature so why the hell would I want to read Tolstoy and Dostoevsky? I couldn't really contribute to the discussions much…it took everything I had to keep myself awake. I did try and read them, I really did, but they were far too high brow for me. I could barely understand them! Reading should be a pleasurable experience not one where you are desperately seeking out a book synopsis online so you can at least look like you've read it. It felt like it was a competition to see who could suggest the most intelligent book as if it was a reflection of your own intellect. They all got so involved. Bless them, they were all so desperate to impress Annabelle, who for some reason appeared to have them all under her control.

Month after month it was the same, no one dared go off-piste with their book suggestions and to be quite honest apart from Annabelle all the other ladies looked dead behind the eyes as soon as we started discussing the book we had supposedly read. I kept on going in the hope that I might be able to strike up a conversation with some of the other ladies. I naively thought I might be able to form some friendships. I was wrong, even the minimal chat at the beginning and end of the sessions followed the same pattern as the books. If Louisa had bought her daughter a Shetland Pony, Annabelle had bought her son a horse. When Tara's son got a first class degree, Annabelle's daughter got a triple first from

Cambridge. Annabelle could better any achievement you would care to mention. What the fuck is wrong with these people? Why is everything a competition and why won't they stand up to that dreadful woman? I have started to chat with a couple of the ladies, but as soon as Annabelle catches their eye, they back off…are they scared of catching flat vowel sounds, worried my north of the Watford Gap habits might rub off on them? I decided things needed to change and if I couldn't liven up the book group I could at least go out in a blaze of glory. They may not want to talk to me, but I was going to make sure they would be talking about me for weeks to come.

Today it's my turn to pick a book and there was never going to be any doubt I was going to pick something outrageous. I'm was clearly not going to make any friends here, so I figured I had nothing to lose. It did seem like a good idea at the time, but now I'm on my way to the village hall I am actually shitting myself. I could be burnt at the stake if this doesn't go well. Annabelle is waiting for me at the door when I arrive. She's tapping her foot impatiently and my stomach starts to churn;

'Hello Julia, I'm really looking forward to hearing all about your book choice this evening. I'm assuming you'll have chosen an author from the north, what with you being one of them.'

'One of them?' The woman is off her fucking head! Through gritted teeth, I tell her it's a surprise and she'll just have to be patient. Annabelle gives me a death stare and half smiles...what the fuck have I done? It seemed like a good idea at the time but now I'm not so sure. I take my usual seat and await my fate;

'Good evening ladies, tonight we have a real treat in store for us. I'd like to ask our newcomer Julia to stand up and tell us all about the book she has chosen for us to read. I'm sure she's chosen really carefully as she wouldn't want to make a bad impression.'

Oh fuck...I can feel my legs starting to tremble as I stand up. I take my chosen book out of my bag and hide the cover. They are all looking at me again and I feel uncomfortable;

'Good evening ladies. Tonight I thought I'd present something a little bit different. Reading should be a joy and I'm sorry to say, that I've felt over the past few months the books we have read have been a little dull. So I thought, let's try something completely different. Something funny, something from an unknown author. With this is mind, the book I have chosen is called Wax Whips and My Hairy Bits. It's a comedy written with women in mind and it follows one woman's disastrous attempts at online dating. It's funny, it's relatable and it is I'm afraid a bit rude.'

I'm standing here holding up the book in complete silence, it's like they are trying to register what I have just said. I look at their faces, they are staring at me in disbelief. Annabelle has gone bright red and looks like she is going to combust and poor Ruth actually looks like she is going to faint. I decide I need to break the silence;

'Come on ladies, at least give it a try…you'll love it, I promise.'

With that they find their voices and I'm met with a torrent of dissatisfaction;

'You want us to read smut?'

'I can't read it if there's swearing, what would the Vicar think?'

'I'm not reading that rubbish, it's most likely poorly written and grammatically incorrect.'

'What makes you think we would want to read that?'

Annabelle eventually finds her incredibly loud voice;

'How dare you bring that…that porn into our lovely book club. This is a quiet, lady like book club. These women are delicate little flowers, they need sensitivity not smut! I knew it was a mistake inviting you to join…you northern people are all the same uncouth and uneducated.'

How fucking dare she, I get the uncouth bit, but I'm every bit as intelligent as anyone in this room. I'm also human, not a robotic country wife with my head up my arse. Just as I'm about to flounce out, a little voice pipes up;

'Actually I think we should give it a try.'

I'm surprised to see it's Ruth speaking up, she's possibly the quietest, mousiest person I have ever met and she's just found her inner lion. Annabelle is furious;

'Oh do be quiet Ruth, what do you know about anything?'

'I know that we've let you dictate what we read for far too long.'

Shit, what have I started? I look around the circle and the ladies finally seem to have some fire in their eyes. I'm taken aback as one by one they change their minds and start to defy Annabelle;

'On reflection, I reckon the vicar will love it. We should read it.'

'I struggle to get into some of the other books we have read, let's go for it and I'll let the grammar go just this once.'

'I could do with a bit of smut in my life, since George had his heart operation I haven't been getting any.'

I laugh out loud at the last comment, poor Tara. Maybe reading the book will give her some ideas. For the first time I can see life in the group and it's really refreshing. However, Annabelle is not finished yet;

'I demand you put that book away and leave the group now! We are not, I repeat not reading that rubbish. I've already told you, this is a sedate group and I will not let you expose my ladies to this debauchery.'

Well that's me told. I get up to leave and Louisa grabs my arm;

'Don't go Julia, we want to read the book and if Annabelle doesn't like it I suggest she leaves'

Annabelle looks furious and I see a flash of fear in some of the ladies eyes.

'Who do you think you are? I started this group from nothing, without me you'd be stuck at home living your sad little lives. I'll go, but you've not heard the last of this. Just you wait until I speak to the vicar. Contrary to what you think he's not going to be happy about this, not one little bit.'

With that, she jumps up from her seat, flings the doors open and leaves. We sit in stunned silence until Ruth started to clap, then all the ladies start to clap and whoop and cheer! Tara finds some plastic cups in the store cupboard and we crack open my bottle of Prosecco. We raise a glass to Wax Whips and my Hairy Bits…The ladies were finally free from Annabelle's tyranny and could read whatever they wanted to. There's a completely different atmosphere in the group as we agree to read the book and meet in a month to discuss it. I feel victorious but I'm sure this is not the last we've heard from Annabelle, she's definitely not the type to go quietly and I wonder what her next move is going to be.

WHAT DID THEY THINK?

Today I'm meeting up with the ladies so we can review the book. We made a pact not to discuss what we have read until today, so I really have no idea what they thought of it. None of them have thrown bread rolls at me in the supermarket so I'm hoping that's a good sign. As I suspected, Annabelle hasn't made things easy for us. After the last book club session she went straight to the Vicar who sent us all this email;

'Book club members, it has been brought to my attention that pornography is being reviewed in the church hall. I cannot allow a church building to be used for such debauched purposes and as from today your book club will not be allowed inside or within a ten metre radius of the church hall. I will pray for you all and may God have mercy on your souls.'

For fucks sake! Annabelle really excelled herself there... pornography, God's mercy? The vicar has clearly consigned us all to hell. She must have scared the poor man to within an inch of his dog collar... I wonder if they sanitised the church hall with holy water? To be honest, I think I'd rather go to hell than spend a minute in Annabelle's company. The woman is Hyacinth Bucket on acid! I'm pleased to say she didn't win. We were expecting a sabotage attempt so we had already made alternative arrangements and decided to meet at Louisa's house. So not only will we be talking about a mucky book, we'll be drinking Prosecco and eating an obscene amount of cake...fuck you Annabelle. Although I do have a niggling feeling that we may have won the battle but not necessarily the war. I get the feeling that every defeat makes Annabelle stronger in her resolve to ultimately win.

I head off to Louisa's house. It's only a short walk away, but I can't help but feel I'm being watched, to be honest I've felt like this since the last meeting. I hear footsteps and spin around, there's nothing except a bush rustling in the wind. I think I must be paranoid... could this be divine retribution? Has the devil come to claim one of his own? I laugh out loud as I think I have watched far too many horror films. I carry on walking and just as I'm calming down I hear footsteps again and then to my horror feel a hand on my shoulder. I'm so scared I leap into the air, pee a little bit and then comes the scream...a full on gut wrenching scream;

'Julia, calm down it's me.'

'Tara? Thank fuck for that, I don't know what's wrong with me. I was convinced I was being followed'

'I've felt like that all week, like someone has been watching me.'

So it's not just me being paranoid, that's a relief. We continue the walk to Louisa's together, I notice we are both looking over our shoulders. This is all very strange. We're not far from Louisa's house when we meet up with Teresa and Belinda. They weren't particularly vocal at the last meeting so I did wonder whether they would actually come tonight. I'm thrilled they are here, it means that everyone who attended the last meeting has defied Annabelle and read the book. It's good to see them doing what they want to do, free from they clutches of that dreadful woman.

We file into Louisa's house, prosecco and snacks in hand and head straight for the kitchen. Louisa and Ruth are waiting for us, Louisa must have started really early as she pissed already;

'Ladies, grab a drink…or two. Let's get this party started.'

I think Louisa must have started the party hours ago. She stumbles towards the front room with us following behind her like expectant puppies. We make ourselves comfortable and feeling a little nervous, I stand up and start to talk;

'Ladies, as you know our book of the month was Wax Whips and My Hairy Bits.'

Before I continue, they start to clap and whoop…they've really been let off the leash now Annabelle has gone.

'I know this book is completely different to anything you've read in the book club before and it must have come as a shock to some of you when I suggested it.

Thank you for taking the time to read it. With it being such a unusual read for you all, I'm curious to know what you thought of it, who wants to start?'

Ruth jumps up straight away, there's not a sign of the little mouse she was a month ago;

'I fucking loved it!'

We all roar with laughter again. I don't think Ruth has ever sworn in her life. She's a church going, choir singing, flower arranging aficionado with a penchant for A-line skirts and thick tights. Ruth is probably a lot younger than she looks but the scary librarian vibe she is so fond of adds years to her. I don't think she's been married all that long and unsurprisingly her husband is the male version of her. They are clearly kindred spirits and both so timid. It wouldn't surprise me at all if they had never consummated their marriage. Once the laughter quietens down Ruth continues;

'I have never laughed so much and learnt so much! The book has really opened my eyes and talks about things I've never even heard of. It's opened up a whole new world of possibilities for me! As you can imagine, Phillip my husband is not the most adventurous in the bedroom department.'

Fuck me, they have had sex…who'd have thought it?

'After reading about Ann's adventures, I really think the time has come to try and spice things up a bit…does anyone know where I can get some handcuffs?'

Well, what can I say, Ruth's husband is clearly up for a

treat.

Next up is Tara, she has been struggling recently. Her husband has been recovering from a heart operation and from what I can gather from the other ladies, he's had her running around like a blue arsed fly, catering to his every whim;

'Oh ladies, what can I say? I have to agree with Ruth, I loved it! I don't think I've ever read so much swearing in my life, but it made me laugh out loud. It cheered me up no end. George is being quite difficult at the moment. I say difficult, he's actually being a complete twat and milking the situation for everything it's worth. Actually, I shouldn't be too hard on him. He's gone through such a difficult time with his health and although I do complain sometimes, all I want is for him to be well again. Reading the book gave me a bit of light relief and that's the first time I can say that about anything I've read from book club. Who'd have thought waxing your lady parts would cause such a rumpus and poor Daniel, he was her perfect man and she blew it. I really need to know what happens with Tom, does anyone know?'

We all burst out laughing at her enthusiasm. I have to resist the temptation to say 'you do know it's not real don't you?' The other ladies are clamouring to give their take on what they have read, so we quickly refill our glasses and move on to Teresa;

'As you know ladies, I'm a stickler for good grammar. This book is written in conversational English so I have to admit some of the grammar did cause my hair to stand on end. However, it was so funny I'll let the grammar go…it's written how some women speak which makes it all the more relatable. The sex scenes had me both laughing and cringing at the same time and I have to admit, as Ann would say, they did make my fanny tingle.'

We are all in hysterics now, Teresa and fanny tingle are definitely not words you would normally put together in the same sentence;

'Excuse me, what are you all laughing at? There's life in this old muff yet I'll have you know!'

Still laughing we head to the kitchen to have a quick break and stuff our faces with cake.

Having consumed copious amounts of cake and probably downed a bit too much prosecco we settle down to listen to the last couple of reviews. Up next is Belinda;

'Well, I can only echo what everyone else has said, I also loved it. What a change from our usual reads. Although like some of the other books we have read, I didn't understand some of the words that were used and had to look them up. My husband nearly passed out when he came across my search history. That'll teach him for being a nosy bastard! It was so much fun and like the others have said it was an education. We definitely need to do this more often, we've chatted more this evening than we have done in years.'

I love that we, as a group of ladies are bonding. I really

feel that I'm finally starting to make some friends, maybe village life is starting to suit me. Last to give their view on the book is Louisa, she's now well and truly pissed so this should be interesting;

'Yep, I fucking loved it too. I think we should take a leaf out of Ann's book...ha! Did you see what I did there? We should all try and spice our love lives up by copying the lady herself. Come on, admit it. I'm not saying all of us, but some of us are stuck in a rut. Be honest with yourselves, when do you get sex? Christmas and birthdays if you are lucky. Your muffs have virtually healed and you wouldn't recognise a fanny tingle if it slapped you in the face.'

'My muff is perfectly fine.' mutters Belinda under her breath.

'Come on girls, let's go for it!'

With that Louisa slumps into her chair and giggles to herself as we sit in stunned silence. I can tell the other ladies are mulling over what Louisa suggested. I really like the idea. There's nothing wrong with having a boost in the bedroom department...keep things fresh and exciting. It's at this moment I start to formulate a plan;

'What do you think of this ladies, I'll write down six scenarios and we all choose one at random. Whatever scenario you select you have to act out with your partner. Don't tell anyone what you've got and we'll meet up next week and discuss what happened...are you in?'

'I'm in' shouts the no longer shy and retiring Ruth. The

excitement in the room is palpable as one by one the other ladies agree to join in. Louisa manages to stagger over to her sideboard and hands me some paper and a pen. I write down:

Intimate hair removal, get that muff gleaming.

Turn him on with sexy lingerie.

Posh restaurant followed by naughtiness in a lift.

Drip candle wax all over him.

Talk dirty to him for a day.

Handcuffs and a horsewhip.

I fold the pieces of paper, pop them in a carrier bag and ask each lady to choose one. We open our tasks in unison and every lady in the room has a smile on her face so I think they are all up for their challenges.

As we finish off the last of the alcohol in the house we all avoid talking about the tasks ahead. We desperately want to, but we can all see the fun in the surprises we are going to have next week when we find out who has done what. Louisa looks like she is just about to fall asleep when she lets out a blood curdling scream... I wonder if she chose handcuffs and horsewhip? We all jump out of our seats and are confused to see her pointing at the window in front of her. We all turn at the same time and see a shadowy figure at the window. It's pouring with rain and they are dripping wet. It takes us a few seconds to realise it's Annabelle, she's completely motionless and staring right at us. Now that is fucking scary, how long has she been standing there? Why is she standing there? Ruth flies out of the front door;

'Fuck off, Annabelle.'

She has definitely found her inner tiger and I think she quite likes using the 'F' word. But Annabelle has gone, disappeared into the night. I'm now convinced someone has been watching me and I think it's her;

'I think she's been following me since the last meeting. I knew I was being watched.'

The others, having felt the same way, agree she has been watching us all. Keeping track of all our movements. The woman seriously needs to get a hobby. Why is she so interested in what we are getting up to? She must be finding it very hard to let go of what she perceives to be 'her ladies' and I think they've all had a lucky escape. We agree to keep a look out for each other and say goodnight excited in the knowledge that the next time we meet up we will all have spiced up our relationships.

TERESA

A week has passed and we've all hopefully been busy working on our challenges. I've bumped into the ladies over the past few days and we've given each other knowing smiles but no one has spilt the beans. I've also bumped into the vicar a couple of times. He always used to be friendly and eager to chat but he barely acknowledged me, just tutted and muttered under his breath and I'm sure he made the sign of the cross as he passed me. I'm quite surprised I'm still allowed in church. I don't know what Annabelle has said about me, but I'm sure it won't be long before they start flicking holy water at me in an attempt to exorcise the smut devil within me. I'm the last to arrive at Louisa's and Ruth is at the door waiting for me;

'For fucks sake Julia, hurry up we're dying to get started, Teresa is going first.'

She looks completely different. The old fashioned skirt has been replaced by jeans, her frilly blouse has been shown the door, replaced with tight fitting black polo neck and she's wearing make-up. She looks ten, no twenty years younger and she is absolutely stunning. It's an amazing, jaw dropping transformation and I'm curious as to what brought it about. I managed to grab the glass of prosecco Ruth thrusts into my hand without spilling it and I take a seat in the living room as Teresa stands up to speak;

'I chose the talking dirty task which was probably quite apt for me considering I love words. I must admit though, I didn't have a clue where to start. Steven has always been the more ebullient out of the two of us.'

I quickly look up what ebullient means on my phone. Personally having met Steven a couple of times I wouldn't have described him as cheerful and full of energy…he comes across as a loud, know it all gobshite who does all the talking. But he could have a good heart and be hung like a donkey so who am I to comment?

'I decided to take it slowly and start off subtly. I woke him up with a cup of coffee and I could tell from the shape of the bed sheet he was standing to attention. This could be the perfect opportunity and maybe it wouldn't take much dirty talk to get him right where I want him…I could have successfully completed my challenge before breakfast if I got this right. I gently whispered 'nice cock' in his ear. I think I must have woken him from a deep sleep because he sat bolt upright looking bewildered; 'Teresa, what did you just say?' So I repeated it slowly putting extra emphasis on the letter K.'

I start to laugh as I imagine our lovely, proper Teresa getting her mouth around the word 'cock'.

'So what did he say?' I really need to know how he

responded to that.

'Well that's the thing, he turned bright red and didn't say anything. He let out a deep sigh, shrugged his shoulders, rolled over and went back to sleep. I did feel slightly offended and all I could think was 'what a waste of a good erection!'

It wasn't the best of starts but Teresa is a determined woman. She's probably right. Steven was most likely in a deep sleep and didn't have a clue what was going on. Maybe he's actually really quite shy and retiring…I can't wait to see how this all pans

'I wasn't going to be put off that easily so I waited until he came downstairs wanting something to eat. 'So tell me Steven, how do you like your eggs? I prefer mine fertilised.' He turned red again and mumbled something about poached being just fine. I thought maybe the egg reference was a bit subtle since my child bearing years are well behind me. I made him his poached eggs and went upstairs to get changed. To try and tempt him, I put on my most cleavage enhancing top. I might be getting on a bit, but I still have fantastic tits. I sauntered into the kitchen, bent over right in front of him so he got an eyeful of my bosom and said 'do you want to plump my pillows?' I perhaps should have waited until he wasn't chewing on a mouthful of food because he started to cough and splutter with a sizeable chunk of egg flying out of his mouth and into my cleavage.'

Poor Teresa, when we should have been sympathetic we

were all pissing ourselves laughing. The thought of her rifling through her cleavage to find a chunk of soggy egg was too much.

'I was starting to feel a little disheartened with my first two attempts at talking dirty falling on truly deaf ears. I decided I'd wait until after lunch before I tried again. The way to Steven's heart was through his stomach and I reasoned if he was full up and content he might take the bait. After spending the morning bending over suggestively in front of him and him moving me out of the way so he could see the television, I made him a huge lunch. Once he had finished and plonked himself back on the sofa. He looked relaxed and happy so I decided to have another go. I draped myself around the door and gestured for him to come to me. 'Do you want to visit my magical pussy palace?' He looked confused for a second, thought about it and replied; 'We've had this conversation before Teresa, we don't want anymore cats'. I seriously could have screamed with frustration and tried to make myself clearer. 'I don't mean cats Steven, I'm thinking about the pussy between my legs.' There's nothing, not even a glimmer of recognition...'Oh come on, surely you know what I mean? I'm talking about my muff, my fanny, my otter's pocket...my fucking vagina!' With that he huffed and puffed, muttering about having to go and mow the lawn...mow the fucking lawn, did he not think my lawn was due for a service?

I can't help but feel sorry for her, she was really giving it her best shot but Steven was proving a tough nut to crack. What was wrong with the man? His lovely wife was handing it to him on a plate and he was ignoring her…fucking outrageous.

'Just when I thought the day couldn't get any worse, there was a knock at the door. It was bloody Annabelle…she really knew how to choose her moments. I didn't know what to say and before I could think of anything, she did all the talking. 'Teresa darling, I hate that there's all this bad blood between us. We've been friends for how many years? We shouldn't let an interloper come between us. She's new to the village, she's not one of us, she's encouraging you to read smut and she's a northerner!' Before I could answer, she pushed a leaflet into my hand…'Here's the details for the new book club I've set up. I just want to get things back to normal as soon as possible, I trust you'll be there.' With that, she just left. She didn't give me the opportunity to answer, she was just gone. I'm starting to think there's something of the night about Annabelle, she's omnipresent and it's seriously beginning to disturb me.'

Well that was strange. Apart from suggesting a book that wasn't on her recommended reading list, I really don't know what I've done to offend her. Does she have that village mentality where anyone from 'the outside' is automatically viewed with suspicion? She clearly has a problem with anyone from the north. Maybe she had a bad experience with a donkey on Blackpool beach as a child or maybe she just a pathological hatred of flat vowel sounds. Whatever the reasons she is determined to make her presence felt.

'After Annabelle left, I thought I'd give the talking dirty a rest until bedtime. I needed time to compose myself and I needed to do some research. I'd just about exhausted my list of rude words and phrases. I don't know what I had expected, but I had hoped my fanny would be tingling and Steven would be insatiable. The rest of the day passed off peacefully. Annabelle didn't reappear and for some reason Steven avoided me. I usually can't shut him up, he's got an opinion about everything and only his opinion is right…the peace and quiet was actually marvellous. It gets to bedtime and he makes us both a cup of cocoa to take to bed…he normally lets me make the bedtime drink so I'm hoping he's finally cottoned on and he's buttering me up for a good old session in the bedroom. We get into bed and drink our cocoa. Steven switches off the light and I lie there…I wait and I wait, but there's no nuzzling into my neck or gentle stroking of my thigh. I decided to give it one last try…'Steven are you still awake?' He grunts his reply 'Yes, why?' I don't know what comes over me but I'm obviously attempting to win a gold medal in talking dirty;

'I want to stroke your length'

'I want to feel you inside me.'

'My favourite number is 69, what's yours?'

I get nothing back and my patience finally snaps…'For fucks sake, do you fancy a shag?' Steven sits bolt upright in bed and switches on the light…'What is wrong with you woman? Have you gone mad? Annabelle was right, reading that smut has turned your head. You've turned into a nymphomaniac. You've never complained about our sex life before. I thought you were happy with Christmas, birthdays and the occasional bank holiday? You need to listen to Annabelle, she talks sense, not like that new woman at the book club filling your head with rubbish. I think I'll sleep in the spare room tonight. I don't know what you'll get up to whilst I'm asleep.' I couldn't help myself ladies, I told him to 'fuck off and shag Annabelle'.

Teresa got up and went into the kitchen to refill her glass. We can't wait to find out what happened next. Steven obviously doesn't know when he's onto a good thing. Teresa is amazing and quite frankly he should be thankful she still wants to sleep with him.

'I'm guessing your wondering how things have been since our argument? Steven is still sleeping in the spare room. I've told him he can stay there until he sees the error of his ways. I don't want to spend the rest of my life being dictated to by the likes of Annabelle and Steven. I've been given a new lease of life. I've realised I've still got a lot of living to do and if he wants me to live the life of a nun he can fuck off. Where the hell does he get off taking advice from that awful woman. I didn't think they had even spoken before and now they are besties…why? I was starting to feel a bit scared of her when she turned up at my house, but not anymore. The gloves are off. If she wants a war that's exactly what she's going to get.'

The ladies break into a spontaneous round of applause. Teresa has come to the realisation that she has to live her best life, have fun and be happy. We move to the kitchen to top up our glasses before the next lady gets up to speak. We all hug Teresa and tell her how fabulous she is. Whatever she decides to do she has all our support. Ruth is bursting to tell us how she got on, so we agree she has to go next. This one should be interesting!

RUTH

Ruth is standing up, glass in hand and ready to go before we can sit down. She really does look fantastic and I can only assume she's had a great time…go girl!

'I can finally reveal that my challenge was to go for a posh meal and then naughtiness in a lift. It took me a little while to figure out how I was going to make this work. My husband Phillip is not really one for going out or socialising. He enjoys his train spotting, but he's not all that good with humans. I think if he never had to suffer human interaction again he would be happy. I'm sure that if our parents hadn't introduced us, he probably wouldn't be married at all…he probably should never have got married in the first place.'

That doesn't sound good…

'Luckily the challenge coincided with our fifth wedding anniversary. It took a lot of persuading but Phillip agreed that we should celebrate at that very expensive Parisian restaurant in town, he even agreed to drive… which wasn't much of a sacrifice as he's tee-total. On the day of the challenge I booked myself in at the beauty parlour and had my eyebrows waxed for the very first time. It fucking hurt ladies, why did nobody tell me!

But...for the first time in my life I no longer have a mono-brow and I'm loving it! I also bought my first set of matching lingerie. When I put on the push up bra for the first time, I couldn't believe I was looking at my tits in the mirror...they looked spectacular, how had I never noticed I had such fantastic tits! To complete my new look, I bought a black cocktail dress. It was split to the thigh and showed a decent amount of cleavage. I was excited getting ready for our meal and I have to admit, ladies, my fanny was tingling. I put my hair up and for the first time in my married life applied some make up. My transformation was complete and even if I do say so myself, I looked hot. All I had to do was reveal it to Phillip.'

This is so good to hear, Ruth is like a butterfly emerging from its cocoon for the first time. I do hope Phillip appreciated it.

'I called Phillip upstairs. He was wearing his standard corduroy trousers, striped shirt and woollen tank top. If I'm honest he really did look like a fifties throwback which could have been cute if he wasn't such a boring bastard. Tonight was my night to relight his fire...not that his fire had ever been lit in the first place and I was determined to go for it. He walked into our bedroom and stopped dead when he saw me...'Ruth, what on earth are you wearing? It's indecent. I can see your body...everyone will be able to see your body. What have you done to your face? You know I prefer you to look natural...what is going on?' I didn't feel the need to justify myself to him. I explained that the meal was booked and I would go with or without him.'

We all cheer, good on you Ruth. Philip really has got his tank top in a twist, he should be delighted that he has such a beautiful, sexy wife.

'I was feeling furious with him by the time we arrived in town, but I had a challenge to complete and I had to focus. The naughtiness in a lift was going to be a problem as the restaurant was on one floor. I had thought maybe I could adapt it and just drag him into the toilets but I wanted to stay true the events in the book. Luckily, I had a brainwave. If we parked on the top floor of the multi storey car park we'd have to get the lift up to get the car when we finished our meal. So that was that sorted and even though Phillip had mightily pissed me off I was starting to feel excited at the prospect. If I could channel my anger into passion Philip would be getting the night of his life.

When we arrive at the restaurant the waiters are fussing all over us, or should I say they are fussing all over me and Phillip does not like it one little bit. I thought I might feel self-conscious wearing such a revealing dress, but it's liberating and I have to admit I was enjoying the attention. I've always been the girl at the back of the room, the awkward one. My parents had me very late on in life. I was a complete surprise and a joy after they had given up all hope of having a child. They were wonderfully kind and caring as I was growing up but unfortunately they were stuck in the past. My Mother was never into fashion, my clothes were comfortable, practical and most of all modest.

She never wore make-up so neither did I. I didn't go anywhere near social media. I wasn't allowed to have a mobile phone, so my whole view of the world was shaped by the four walls in which I lived. As I was an only and much wanted child, they were over protective. There was no question of me having a boyfriend. Philip was the son of their close friends and we grew up together. I always wondered whether the long term plan was for us to get married. He was the perfect match in the eyes of my parents. He wasn't exciting or dynamic and I guess they thought he would never lead me astray or break my heart. I found marriage to Phillip exciting at first…I didn't know anything different. I was happy to be the dutiful wife. I cooked, I cleaned and I pulled my nightie up every so often for a quick shag. I have to be honest with myself and admit that for a long time I've felt like something has been missing. I was hoping that this challenge would bring some much needed spice into my life, but Phillip wasn't playing ball just yet.

We order our food and I'm tempted to go for oysters like Ann did in the book, but like Ann I don't think I could stomach them and Phillip would be absolutely horrified. He likes his food the same way as he likes his sex…bland. As we are eating I ask Phillip why he doesn't like my new look, his answer doesn't really surprise me…'It's too much Ruth, all that flesh on show and you don't need all that muck on your face'. I lean forward and thrust my cleavage at him…'Don't you like my tits Phillip?' 'For God's sake Ruth, put them away. People are watching…you'll put them off their food.'

The cheeky bastard! I was certainly not going to put them away, I was enjoying every moment of my new found freedom, no one had ever looked at me before and I was going to milk it while it lasted. As we start on our desert, I decide to step it up a notch...the conversation hasn't exactly been flowing and I've been necking back prosecco at quite a pace. I slip off my shoe and start to rub my foot up and down his leg. He's not reacting so I don't think he's noticed...there's only one thing left to do, my foot heads straight for his cock. I see his back stiffen...it's the only thing that is stiffening, his cock is not reacting in the slightest. He doesn't say a word but pushes his chair back from the table so I can't reach...fucking spoilsport. This is proving to be a lot harder than I thought. Phillip won't even make eye contact with me whilst we are finishing our desert which is pretty awkward, but nothing compared to what happened next...'

The room is silent as we wait, desperate to know what she could be talking about. Ruth takes a long slow slip of her drink and I have to resist the temptation to tell her to get on with it.

'I felt like someone was watching me and I noticed a familiar pair of eyes peering over a menu on the table opposite us.'

'Annabelle' we all shout in unison.

'It was indeed. I didn't know where to put myself and tried to ignore her until it was too late. She got up walked over to our table and slammed her book club leaflet down next to me. Not a word was spoken. It was all very strange and a bit fucking surreal. Philip however didn't seem at all surprised and if you ask me he almost seemed pleased to see her. I think he saw her as some kind of back up. Before I could screw the leaflet up, Phillip took it and put it in his pocket...'I'll keep hold of this Ruth, you never know you might need it, you need to listen to Annabelle, Ruth. She's a good role model for you, she keeps you grounded...she encourages you to behave.' I can't believe he's talking to me like I'm a naughty child and I can feel my cheeks starting to glow red. He needn't have bothered keeping hold of the leaflet, there was no fucking way I was going to Annabelle's book group. Seeing her there in the restaurant had made me lose my focus a little bit, nothing screams passion killer more than being on the receiving end of Annabelle's death stare. I needed to get the challenge back on track, so as we left the restaurant I gave Philip's arse a little squeeze. I thought he might be starting to warm up a little bit as we held hands all the way back to the carpark. Philip headed towards the stairs which was definitely not in the plan. 'Come on Philip, lets get in the lift. These shoes are killing me, I'll never make it up all those stairs.' Ever the gentleman he agreed and I could throw everything into completing my challenge. As the lift doors shut I threw my arms around Philips neck and tried to kiss his ear. 'Come on Ruth, there's a time and a place for everything and this isn't it.' I wasn't going to be put off so I tried again...'Oh Phillip, where's your sense of adventure?' This time he did let me kiss him and with that I lost all my inhibitions, my fanny was tingling and I was ready for action. I grabbed his hand and put it between my legs…'Finger me Phillip.' I looked up at his face and I could see all the colour draining out of it. He pushed me away and could barely contain his disgust…'What has happened to you Ruth? Annabelle said this would happen if you associated with that brazen northern hussy from the book club. She's a bad influence on you and I forbid you from seeing her again.' I was actually speechless. I threw myself at him, couldn't have been more blatant and rather than take me up on my offer he's quoting fucking Annabelle. We didn't speak at all on the drive home. Phillip went straight to bed, but before he went up he handed my Annabelle's leaflet and told me to seriously consider joining her book club as it would be good for me…I told him to go fuck himself.'

We are all shedding tears of laughter again. I love the new Ruth.

'I didn't sleep all that well. I had so much running through my head. I didn't want to be a quiet, dutiful housewife…I wanted to live my life and have fun. I didn't want to be stuck in the corner anymore and I wasn't going to be the little mouse that everyone ignored for a moment longer. When Phillip came downstairs, he was carrying a bag…'I've decided to go and stay with my parents for a few days, you need time to reflect on your behaviour…you need to listen to Annabelle.' Can you guess what I said to him ladies?'

'Fuck off Phillip' we all shout in unison.

'How did you guess? All my life people have told me what to do, how to think and what to wear. I'm not that person anymore. As soon as Phillip had got into his car and driven off I went upstairs, emptied my wardrobe and threw the whole lot in the bin. I jumped straight onto my laptop and ordered a whole new wardrobe in keeping with a 29 year old. I made a vow to myself that I would never again wear American tan tights. It was liberating! I booked a hair appointment and I might even have a spray tan next. It was only when he had gone I realised how dull my life with Phillip actually was. Suddenly I could watch what I wanted on the television…I would never have to sit through another boring documentary about the life span of a mayfly ever again. If Phillip was going to come home he would have to make some changes himself…radical changes which included a personality transplant. However after speaking to his Mother I realised that would never happen. She called me as soon as he arrived home and had given her his version of attempts. I'd say she was furious but she was angrier than that. In her opinion I didn't deserve Phillip. She always knew he should have married Esther from church. I had gone off the rails, I didn't appreciate him and I was turning into a brazen hussy…can you guess what I said to her?'

Once again in complete unison we shouted 'Fuck of Phillip's Mum'.

'You are correct…again! Horrified by my treatment of her son and my use of 'swears' she immediately called my Mother who in turn, called me. I took a deep breath as I answered the phone, but my Mum completely surprised me...'Ruth, I've just had Felicity on the phone and she's told me what's been going on with you and Phillip. My darling girl, live your life and be happy. If Phillip doesn't make you happy and if he and his parents are trying to control you in anyway, then you are more than justified in telling them all to fuck off. If that dreadful woman calls here again I shall be telling her to fuck off myself!' That was the first time in my whole life I had heard my Mum swear and it was brilliant. So that's me ladies, I failed my challenge but found myself.'

Before Ruth sits down we all hug her, what a fantastic woman. Phillip doesn't know what he's lost. We have another quick break before Belinda tells us how she got on with her challenge.

BELINDA

Belinda stays seated to tell us all about her challenge. She's hurt her foot and won't tell us how she did it. I'm assuming it's something to do with her challenge… finally it looks like somebody had some fun!

'For my challenge, I choose intimate hair removal…I had to get my muff gleaming. I wasn't too worried about the task. I'd always kept my bush nicely trimmed so this was the next step really. When I did my weekly shop, I put some hair remover cream in the trolley and giggled to myself the whole way around the supermarket. I don't know why, but I felt really naughty…it was my turn to be an erotic Goddess and I was going to go the full mile, flaps and all. I've been very lucky with my Geoff. We may be in our sixties but sex has never been a problem. He's always been up for a bit of fanny fun.'

We are all howling with laughter by this point. I'm never going to be able to look at Geoff in the same way again. Who would have thought that sweet, white haired Geoff was a sex machine. As for Belinda, I'm shocked. It's refreshing to hear her talking so frankly. She comes across as quite straight laced and proper… never judge a book by its cover!

'I tell you ladies, there's not much me and Geoff haven't tried in our forty years together. If there's anything you ever need to know, just ask me. I have a wealth of knowledge. Think of me as your sexual Agony Aunt.'

I think we might be getting too much information now. There are some things we really don't need to know and some things we wouldn't want to ask Belinda about.

'When I told Geoff about my challenge, he was well up for it, he couldn't wait to see the end result. To be honest, it was like all his Christmases had come at once. He had hinted at me braving the shave before, but to be honest I didn't take him seriously. As soon as I got home from the supermarket, he took my coat, patted me on the arse and told me to get to work on my shaven haven. He even asked if I wanted any help applying the cream, an offer I politely declined as a woman has to maintain a certain amount of mystery. I went upstairs and stripped from the waist down. Now how was I going to do this? I applied cream to everywhere I could see clearly, but the undercarriage was going to be a problem. I tried using a mirror, but I couldn't hold the mirror and apply the cream at the same time…co-ordination never was my strong point. So I decided that the best course of action would be to put one leg on the bath and then I'd get a better view of my lady garden and be able to apply the cream more accurately. I got myself into position and although I wobbled a little bit I was confident this was the right thing to do. I couldn't have been more wrong. As well as my co-ordination being a bit off, my balance wasn't great either. Before

I could react I slipped and fell backwards. I felt myself falling backwards but I couldn't right myself and I don't know how I did it, but as I fell my big toe wedged itself into the cold tap. My back hit the floor with such a thud Geoff came running upstairs…'Belinda, love are you alright?' He stopped dead and burst out laughing when he saw me. I was flat on my back and half naked with my creamed up muff on display for all to see. 'Come on, I'll help you up.' 'Look at my toe Geoff, I can't get up!' He started laughing again and I was furious. 'Don't just stand there, do something…pass my a towel so I can this fucking cream off.' He's still laughing as he throws me a towel. 'Now try and pull my toe out of the tap so I can get up.' Geoff pulls and he pulls, but my toe is not budging. I send him to the kitchen to get some butter. To my horror even though both my toe and the tap are liberally slavered in Lurpak nothing happens.

I'm starting to feel extremely anxious, especially when Geoff suggests calling the fire brigade. 'Do not under any circumstances call the fire brigade. My minge is on display, my toe is stuck in the tap…the last thing I need is to be making small talk with a procession of young, attractive fire fighters trying not to laugh as they try and work out how the fucking hell they are going to get me out of this mess.' Suddenly Geoff has a brainwave…'I need to cut it off.' He can see the horror my face as I immediately assume he's talking about my toe…'The tap, if I can cut the tap off, then at least you can get up and we can decide what to do with you.' I reluctantly agree and he's goes off to find his saw. As I'm lying there waiting for him to come back, I decide I will never ever try to de-fuzz my fanny again. It obviously wasn't mean to be. Poor Geoff was going to be ever so disappointed, but I'm sure I can make it up to him.'

My mind boggles at the thought of what she's going to do to Geoff to make up for his shaven haven disappointment.

'After switching off the water Geoff sets about sawing through the tap. It doesn't take him too long and he's done...I can't tell you what a relief it was. Finally I can put my leg down, cramp was setting in and I was freezing cold. Geoff brings me a pair of loose joggers and helps me downstairs. We sit in the living room for what feels like an eternity, both of us starting at the tap perched on top of my toe. It's starting to pulsate and I'm beginning to worry I'll never be able to get it off. I'll be forever be known as the little old lady who walks around the village with a tap on her toe. It's the sort of thing they used to write nursery rhymes about...

There was an old woman who liked things just so

Her bush was overgrown and just had to go

She slipped on the bath, which wasn't a laugh

As she has a tap for a toe now'

There isn't a dry eye in the house when Belinda finishes her poem...who knew she was a poet? I can't see it turning up on the English curriculum anytime soon but it certainly made us laugh.

'Having acknowledged that I really did have to get the

tap off, we decide the best course of action was to go to the local Walk-in centre. I put a sock on, so it covers up my misfortune. I don't particularly want the world to see what a complete twat I've been. Thankfully the Walk-in centre is quiet and it's not long before Geoff is helping me hobble towards a consultation room. I pull my sock off and the nurse tries her best to stifle her giggle. She tells us she needs to get a colleague to have a look as she's not to sure what to do. When she bring two other nurses back with her I know that I'm the talk of the Walk-in centre. They gently try and pull the tap off...do they not think we've tried that? Then they try using washing up liquid (I didn't think of that) and praise be with one strong tug it pops off and my toe emerges as red and swollen as a baboon's arse. I can't stop thanking them, they have liberated my foot and I will be eternally grateful. My toe is strapped up and I'm warned it is going to be painful for a few days...I can live with that. Geoff helps me hobble towards the exit and guess who is waiting for me?'

Once again we find ourselves shouting 'Annabelle' in unison.

'Yep, Annabelle. Hanging around like a vulture circling its prey. I tried to ignore her but she got up and followed us out...'Yoo hoo, Belinda.' I ignored her and we carried on walking. But you know Annabelle, she never takes no for an answer. She overtook us and stopped us dead in our tracks. 'Belinda, here's a leaflet for my new book club, I expect you'll be there.' The bare faced cheek of the woman. 'No Annabelle, I won't be there. Please leave me alone.' Rather than respond to me, she turned to Geoff...'I'm disappointed in you Geoff. Why have you let it go this far? I take it she was trying one of the silly challenges from the book. You need to have a word with her Geoff, she'll be out of control like the others if you don't take her in hand.' Can you guess what Geoff said to her?'

'Fuck off Annabelle' we screech through tears of laughter.'

'With that she vanished. I don't know where she comes from or where she disappears to, but she is becoming a massive pain in the arse. Obviously I put her leaflet straight in the bin. I found the original group hard work, why on earth would I want to go back now?

When we got back home Geoff waited on me hand and foot, he was so sweet and really appreciated my attempt to give him the shaven haven he'd secretly longed for. He was so sympathetic he even offered to get a sack, back and crack wax...I told him it was a very sweet offer but there was absolutely no need. To be honest, I'm not sure his old balls would cope with it. As for my lady garden it was a bit of a disaster zone. As I'd wiped the cream off so quickly it had worked in some areas but not others, so for now I'd have to make do with a patchy muff which looked like an art experiment gone wrong. Although failed my challenge, it wasn't a completely wasted exercise. Geoff and I agreed the thought of doing something new was really exciting and even though our love life was already fantastic we would try and experiment at least once a month.'

Some of the ladies are looking a little envious of Belinda. I think it's brilliant that her an Geoff have an active sex life well into their sixties. Why should sex stop as you get older? We decide to take another quick break before Tara gets up to speak. As we help ourselves to more alcohol and cake the topic of conversation has moved away from our challenges and onto Annabelle. She seems to be stalking every single member of the group. Maybe losing her grip on the original group has tipped her over the edge. Who knows?

TARA

Tara looks a little nervous as she stands up to tell us all about her challenge. She's not a great public speaker and this is a bit of an ordeal for her. I do hope it worked out well for Tara, but given the look on her face I'm not going to hold my breath. We give her a clap of encouragement and she starts to speak;

'For my challenge, I had to try and turn George on with sexy lingerie. I was so relieved that I had chosen one of the tamer challenges. As you know George is recovering from heart surgery and he has been quite frail for some time now.'

We all nod sympathetically but our sympathy is with Tara not George. Having spoken to a couple of the other ladies, the general consensus was that George was well and truly swinging the lead. He had a minor heart operation months ago and looks in perfect health every time he goes to the pub with his friends.

'I've always been quite traditional in the underwear department so I didn't quite know where to start. I had a look online and oh my goodness, I'm a lady of a certain age. There was no way I could wear some of the thing I saw. Thongs, G-strings, crotchless knickers, peek-a-boo bras...they didn't look comfortable or practical. They showed everything...why bother wearing underwear at all if you are just going to wear a piece of string?'

We all start to laugh. They are not supposed to be practical or comfortable...string is actually a thing Tara. Poor love, I think this challenge is going to be really hard work.

'It's not funny, I was starting to get really stressed by it all. Even if I'd wanted to wear a crotchless body stocking...which I didn't. I don't think George would have been able to cope with the excitement. He struggles to put his slippers on most days so I knew I had to be careful. I decided that rather than risque lingerie I would try a sexy nightdress. It took me an age to find what I was looking for. I had an idea in my head and I was absolutely set on it. I wanted to go for a 1950's Doris Day look...you must know what I mean? So I bought a long pink chiffon nightdress with a feather trim on the sleeves and the hem. I managed to get a matching dressing gown and heeled open toed slippers also with a feather trim. When it arrived, I waited until George was having one of his naps and tried it on. It had the desired effect. It made me feel like a movie star and you know those fanny tingles you keep talking about... something definitely began to stir.'

Well that's promising. Tara obviously feels confident in feathery, pink chiffon and self confidence is sexy. I'm inwardly cheering Tara on, she desperately needs a bit of fun.

'So the next decision I have to make is just when do I give George his surprise. I can't really leave it until bedtime because the poor thing is so tired by the end of the day he just wants to collapse into bed. He has been so brave dealing with his heart issues and his surgery.'

I really want to shout 'Tara, he's bullshitting you' but I don't think it would do any good. She's completely blind to his behaviour. George can do no wrong…she completely and utterly adores him.

'On the day in question, I got up early and had long soak in the bath. I left George sleeping as long as I could because I thought the rest would do him good. As a special treat and to try and get him in the mood I took him breakfast in bed. Nothing exciting, just porridge and fresh orange juice. He has to watch his diet now and he's very strict about what he'll eat.'

Wrong again Tara, when my husband last saw him in the pub he was tucking into a full English Breakfast…I don't think he's as worried about his cholesterol as he's making out.

'When he'd finished his breakfast, I plumped up his pillows, took away his breakfast tray and told him to stay put because once he'd finished his breakfast I had a surprise for him. This seemed to pique his interest… he sounded excited as he asked if I'd got him a new laptop. He'd been spending a lot of time on his old one since he'd been ill and it was becoming quite unreliable. I do hope he wasn't going to be disappointed. As for me, I was starting to get really excited. For the first time in my life I actually felt naughty. I quickly changed into my seduction outfit. I did struggle to walk in the slippers a little…you know me ladies I never wear heels. So I had to spend a bit of time walking up and down the hallway to get my balance. Then, with a squirt of perfume and a splash of lipstick I was ready to go. Using my most seductive voice I call out to George…'George, switch off the television, I have your surprise.' He answered immediately; 'will do love, what is it? Is it my new laptop? And what's wrong with your voice are you choking on something?' I felt like backing out at this point. I took a deep breath and decided to carry on, I'd come this far and was damned if I was going to back out now.'

'I decided to work my new look and started off by just showing my fluffy slippered leg first. I draped it around the door and moved it up and down the door frame as sexily as I could. 'Tara? What the hell have you got on your feet? What are you playing at? Get yourself and my new laptop in here.' Oh shit, it suddenly dawns on me that I have probably massively fucked up. I float into the bedroom and feebly shout 'surprise'. George looks confused…'Very nice love, now where's my laptop?' 'There is no laptop George…I'm the surprise. I thought you might like my sexy new look. It's been so long since we've been intimate I thought this might get you going.' He is not happy, not happy at all…'You've dressed up like a demented flamingo to get me to sleep with you? Did you look in the mirror Tara, do you have any idea how ridiculous you look? Have you know idea what

I've been through…my heart wouldn't take it or are you trying to get rid of me?' I felt bloody awful. I hadn't thought this through. I'd got carried away with the thought of dressing like a 1950's film star, I got carried away with the romance of it all. I'd put my needs before George's, I was putting him at risk to satisfy my own needs. I felt furious at myself, how could I have been so selfish. I had let George down.'

I open my mouth to speak, but Ruth shakes her head and mouths 'don't'. I'll hold my tongue for now, but George is really pissing me off. He's made her think she's in the wrong and trampled on the confidence she had tried so hard to build up…what a selfish twat.

'After I got changed I went downstairs where George was putting on his coat. I apologised profusely for getting it so wrong. George was having none of it. he stormed out of the house for a walk, he said he needed to clear his head.'

Needed to go to the pub more like. I would put money on him popping into the local, stuffing his face with unhealthy food and downing copious amount of beer.

'As soon as he had gone. I put my new outfit in the bin. I never want to see pink chiffon again…why oh why did I even think it would be remotely ok? It was obviously too soon for George. I clearly underestimated the affect his heart surgery had had on him. I decided to go online and buy his new laptop. Since he'd been virtually housebound his laptop was his link to the outside world. He deserved the best I could afford and I wanted to show him that I did genuinely care.'

By this point I feel like banging my head against a brick wall. Why can't Tara see that he's taking advantage of her sweet and kind nature.

'It's getting late when George eventually gets home. I was starting to worry that he'd had a heart attack and was lying in a ditch somewhere. I can't tell you how relieved I was when I heard his key in the door. I rush to greet him and was shocked to see he was not alone... anyone care to guess who was with him?'

It's starting to become a bit of a habit but we all shout 'Annabelle' again!

'Yes, Annabelle. I held open the door as they both walked straight past me and headed into the sitting room. I wasn't sure what I was expected to do, did I join them or wait until I was invited? I was so curious I decided to follow them. Annabelle had made herself right at home...'Do sit down Tara.' Thank you very much Annabelle, it's not like it's my house or anything. I sit in silence as Annabelle starts her speech;

'Tara. What have you been up to? I met poor George on the lane and he was in quite a state, I was quite worried that he was going to have a heart attack at any moment. He said you were behaving inappropriately. Dressing up like a hussy to try and entice him to do things he shouldn't be doing given the state of his health. What has happened to you? The Tara I knew would never have risked George becoming ill again. I know it's not all your fault. You've been influenced by that northerner.

She's made you like this…think back Tara. Before you met her, you would never have considered reading a smutty book. Look at you now, almost finishing poor George off because you've had your head turned by filth. Why change Tara, you're happy here with George. You have a nice, quiet life why do you want things to be different? I've set up a new book club, come and join me again and let's put this silliness behind us. Let's get things back to normal Tara'.

She mentioned me again 'the northerner'. By this point I am at a loss as to what to think. I don't give a shit what she thinks about me. These ladies are my friends and I'm not going to let her manipulate them.

'She handed me the same leaflet she'd given the others and let herself out. George jabbed his finger at the leaflet in my hand and told me I needed to take Annabelle up on her offer. I have changed apparently and he wants his old Tara back. I felt absolutely awful. I wanted to make George happy but I enjoy spending time with you ladies. Reading that book was one of the funniest experiences I've ever had and I don't really want to go back to Annabelle and her deathly boring book club. But I don't think I have any choice. George doesn't want me to see you anymore and I need to put his needs first. I'm so sorry ladies. I can't tell you how much I've enjoyed spending time with you all.'

We cannot let this happen. Both George and Annabelle are trying to manipulate her for their own ends;

'Tara, don't make any hasty decisions. I think we are

all agreed there is something funny going on with Annabelle.'

'Too fucking right' shouts Ruth.

'We need to get to the bottom of it. We need to work together to find out what is going on. She clearly hates me, but I'm not sure that's all that's driving her in her crusade. Why is she so keen to get our husbands on side? I'm confident she won't approach mine, he's far too northern and she wouldn't want to be tainted by his accent. Before you make any decisions, give us the chance to uncover exactly what she is up to. I'm going to tell you something now Tara and you don't have to believe me. My husband has seen George on more than one occasion tucking into a breakfast in the pub and we are not talking porridge and fresh orange juice. Tara looks at me with disbelief;'

'No, you must be mistaken. I told you, George is terribly careful about what he eats.'

'I've seen him too Tara.' Belinda says in almost a whisper.

'Me too' chips in Ruth.

Tara looks like she is about to cry…but she's not, she's furious.

'So what is the bastard up to. He has driven me to despair about his food, constantly lecturing me about cholesterol and calories. I put butter on his crumpets one morning and he accused me of trying to kill him. I bet that's where he went when he stormed out, straight to the pub to stuff his face. I don't believe for one minute Annabelle 'accidentally' bumped into him, it's very convenient isn't it…he storms out and the first person he bumps into is Annabelle. I think they're plotting something…but what ladies?'

Thankfully we've managed to keep Tara onside. It's just me a Louisa left now to talk about our challenges and Louisa is up next.

LOUISA

Louisa is pissed again, so this one is definitely going to be fun. I'm finding it a bit difficult to concentrate now though. Annabelle is right there at the front of my mind. I really need to know what her end game is. Is she just bitter and twisted because the group went against her, or is there something else, something we don't know about. It really is a kaleidoscope of mystery. For fucks sake, Louisa is struggling to get out of her chair… how much has she had?

'Good evening lovely ladies. I suppose you all want to know what my challenge was? Well I'm not telling you…only joking! For my challenge, I got handcuffs and a horsewhip. My John was absolutely made up when I told him. Like the lovely Belinda I have absolutely no complaints in the bedroom department. John has always been well up for it, he's never had any inhibitions. We even did it in the store cupboard in the church hall once…shhh don't tell the Vicar.'

I knew this one was going to be entertaining!

'Anyway, where was I? Oh yes handcuffs and a horsewhip. Well, there's not much to say really…I handcuffed John to the bed and then whipped his arse with a horsewhip I nicked from the stables and he fucking loved it. Can I sit down now I feel a bit dizzy.'

No sooner does Louisa sit down than she springs back up again;

'I forgot to say, after I had given John a good thrashing with the horsewhip, there was a knock at the door. John pulled on his boxer shorts and answered it half naked with one wrist still in the handcuffs. I don't even need to say who its was, but I'll give you a clue...evil, old witch.'

We don't even bother to shout Annabelle, we know exactly who she's talking about.

'When John answered the door, she took one look at his handcuffed wrist and tried to give him the same old spiel she gave the others...I'm being led astray, I'm reading smutty books, I'm associating with people from the north, blah, blah, blah. John doesn't take any shit. He told her that if reading a smutty book was responsible for the quality shag he's just had I could read as many as I wanted. Her mouth his the fucking floor apparently, he's still laughing about it now. Can I sit down now or I think I might be sick.'

Teresa rushes to the kitchen and brings Louisa a bucket just in case. I'm up next but before I can get up to speak we hear the front door open...we all look at each other wondering, yet at the same time knowing who it was going to be. Before anyone can speak her name, the sitting room door flies open. I knew Louisa should have locked the front door. Annabelle stands there completely motionless and looking absolutely furious. Her eyes dart around the room, she's doing a mental head count to check who is here. It's Teresa who speaks first;

'What do you want Annabelle, we've all had more than enough of this bullshit now.'

Annabelle's lips twitch and she starts to speak;

'Swearing now are we Teresa...I had hoped your husband would have talked some sense into you. Ruth, I'm surprised to see you here and as for you Tara how could you leave poor vulnerable George on his own whilst you discuss things of a sexual nature. What if he falls over and can't reach his phone? He'll be all alone, gasping for breath on the floor whilst you are discussing things women of your age really shouldn't be talking about

That's a pretty low blow trying to scare Tara into leaving...it doesn't work, Tara stays put. This is the clearly the final straw for Annabelle. She points at me barely able to contain her fury;

'This is all your fault. Who do you think you are coming to our village and filling their minds full of your nonsense. We don't need you or want you here. So why don't you take yourself back to that northern hovel where you belong. When are you going to realise that you are not wanted here?'

Belinda has to hold me back as all I want to do it give her a slap.

'See, see how aggressive she is. You all saw that, she went for me. She was clearly dragged up and she wants to drag you down with her. You are better than this ladies. Better than a violent northern guttersnipe who is hell bent on bringing you down to her level. Come with me, leave now and lets get back to normal.'

Annabelle turns to leave and all the ladies (apart from Louisa who is fast asleep) get up and walk after her. For one horrible moment I think they are actually going with her. I should have had more faith. They follow her to the door and as soon as she steps over the threshold they quickly shut and lock it. Ruth however can't leave it at that and has to shout 'fuck off Annabelle' through the letterbox. We all file into the kitchen to fill up our glasses and eat cake to help with the shock. I don't feel like recounting my challenge. I think we've got bigger fish to fry and my challenge can wait for another day;

'It's my turn to talk to you about my book challenge, but I think we have more important things to deal with. This situation with Annabelle is getting out of hand. She clearly hates me which is fine, I'm not all that keen on her either. But why does she want to control the rest of you? Why is she going so far as to try and turn your husbands against you? We need to find out what this is all about ladies and we need to do it now.'

'What do you suggest we do?' Asks Ruth excitedly.

'We need to each of us go online and do some research. Look at her social media, maybe even contact her friends. Someone must know what she's all about. Now who is friends with her on Facebook?'

I'm met with a wall of silence, not one of us was friends with her on Facebook...not much of a surprise really!

'Right we need a plan. Tara, get onto Facebook and send Annabelle a friend request. I think she sees you as the weakest link so she'll probably accept, she'll think you are coming around to her way of thinking and it will be a moment of triumph for her. Everyone else, just start digging. We know that Annabelle moved to the village about thirty years ago...where was she before and does anyone know her maiden name?'

Again, I'm faced with silence. Annabelle appears to be a bit of an enigma. We seem to be glued to our screens for hours when Tara shrieks excitedly;

'Julia, you were right! She's accepted my friend request. I can see her posts and her friends.'

We excitedly gather around Tara's phone as she scrolls through Annabelle's photos. There's nothing particularly exciting just inspirational memes, dog pictures and posts about the church (no wonder the Vicar is so keen on her), until eventually, we come to an old photo of Annabelle and her sister. It does come as a bit of a surprise to the other ladies, they have known Annabelle for years and she has never mentioned having a sister or having any family at all. Conveniently she has tagged her in the photograph so we have a name, Martha Braithwaite. Now unless Martha is married, this could be Annabelle's maiden name and the breakthrough we've been looking for. I know exactly what we need to do;

'Tara, send her a friend request and then send her a message. Tell her we planning a surprise party for her sister to thank her for everything she has done for us. You need to say that the party is going to have a family theme and we want to put a memory book together. Anything she can tell us about Annabelle growing up would be fantastic.'

Tara sends the message and we wait. We've not uncovered much about Annabelle on the internet just an article written by the local newspaper on the original book club. It's the most gushing, vomit inducing piece of journalism I think I've have ever read...how does she charm these people, do they not see through her straight away? There's obviously another side to Annabelle that I haven't seen. I think she charms people, reels them in and then terrifies them into not leaving her side. All the ladies in this room are bright, intelligent and articulate yet she had them cowering in fear and now Annabelle feels she's losing control over them she's moved onto their husbands...why? Tara's phone pings and we all hold our breath...'

'It's her, it's Martha. She's messaged me back. Oh, this looks interesting. I'll read it to you.'

'Hi Tara,

Thanks for messaging me regarding my sister. I'm not sure I'll be that much help. Annabelle doesn't keep in touch with the family apart from the occasional Christmas card. We were born and brought up in Blackpool, Lancashire. Annabelle is a Braithwaite by birth. I'm not sure she would appreciate you mentioning her northern roots, she hated living in Blackpool. From about five years old she used to practise her vowel sounds, even at that age the northern accent offended her. Annabelle did everything she could do distance herself from northern culture...you would never see her eating a Lancashire hotpot. She taught herself to cook so she wouldn't have to eat 'that northern muck' as she called it. Annabelle refused to do all the things we loved growing up, she wouldn't go near the donkeys on the beach and heaven forbid any of her friends ever invited her to go to the Pleasure Beach. I think she saw everyday as one day closer to leaving the north. She worked really hard at school and she was elated the day she left Blackpool to attend a university down south. From the moment she left she turned her back on us. When she graduated she wouldn't invite our parents to the ceremony for fear of their accents showing her up...she broke their hearts and I will never forgive her for that. You seem quite fond of her, so maybe she has changed. Please be wary of her. She's not what she seems and she won't stop to get what she wants. Annabelle doesn't care who shetramples over to achieve success. I'm sorry I couldn't be more help.

Martha'

Fucking hell! Annabelle is a northerner...Annabelle Braithwaite. We can't stop laughing, no wonder she hated me. I reminded her of who she was and where she came from. She's built up this whole back story and I think she saw me as a threat to that. Maybe she was afraid if she heard my accent she would drop a vowel and her cover would be blown. This is hilarious, Annabelle is a Sandgrown'un. She's not just northern, she comes from the Las Vegas of the north... that's hilarious. Is that why she doesn't want the other ladies associating with me, is she scared they'll catch the northern and unmask her? She must be pretty desperate if she's resorting to using their husbands to try and stop them seeing me. She obviously wants to keep her true heritage secret but I can't help but think there's something more to it.

'So ladies, Annabelle is not who she says she is. The question is, what are we going to do about it, do we need to do anything at all?

Ruth speaks first 'I think we should go straight round there and tell her to fuck off...the northern twat...no offence Julia.'

'No offence taken Ruth. I think we should confront her with what we've found out. Maybe if she knows that we know she might leave us alone.'

The ladies nod in agreement. So that's what we are going to do. Tomorrow morning we are going to meet outside Annabelle's house and confront her about her secret northern past. Maybe this is the breakthrough we need and we can finally move on from Annabelle's tyranny. As we are leaving Louisa's husband returns from the pub so we fill him in on what's happened and give him instructions to tell Louisa to meet us at

11.00am outside Annabelle's house. I don't think I've ever seen someone laugh as much and we have to swear him to silence. We can't have this plastered all over the internet before we get the chance to speak to her. He promises to keep quiet and let us have our moment... I get the feeling he may well be hiding behind a bush tomorrow so he can enjoy the fireworks.

ANNABELLE

I didn't sleep too well last night. My mind was full of what I was going to say to Annabelle today. I genuinely wish her no ill will, I just want this nonsense to stop. Why is it when groups of women get together there is always fucking drama. Surely we would be better off supporting each other rather than pitting women against women...do we not have enough shit to deal with without attacking each other? Hopefully once today is over and done with peace will be restored to the village. I'm the first to arrive at Annabelle's house. It's eerily quiet with not a sound to be heard apart from the wind gently rustling the leaves on the trees. Even the birds are quiet...they've probably sensed there's going to be trouble ahead with Annabelle and fucked off even further south. I'm in half a mind to just drop it and go home, but I can see the other ladies heading towards me. The others have been filling Louisa in on everything she missed when she fell asleep and Ruth is jumping up and down like an excited puppy. There's so much excited chatter, we need to calm down and decide what we are going to say;

'Ladies. We need a plan.'

'No we don't' shouts Ruth 'We just need to tell her to fuck off.'

I'm starting to wish Ruth had never learnt to swear. We need to approach the situation calmly or it's just going to turn into a slanging match.

'I think we need to knock on the door and when she answers, we tell her that we know all about her background. We need to make her an offer...if she leaves us and out husbands alone, in return we won't tell anyone about her northern roots. I think that sounds fair don't you?'

'Too fucking fair.' Says a shocked Louisa...she's still trying to get her head around everything that happened when he was asleep.

'Are you ready ladies?'

They all shout 'yes' apart from Ruth who predictably shouts 'too fucking right'. We are just about to head up to Annabelle's front door when a delivery van arrives. The driver approaches us with a large parcel;

'Alright ladies. I've got a parcel for Madam and I'm running really late...could you give it to her please?'

I take the parcel, why did he call her Madam? I know she thinks a lot of herself but to have delivery drivers addressing her as Madam is taking things a little far... She'll be Lady Annabelle before we know it. We all look at the address on the package and strangely it is addressed to 'Madam' and the first line of the address is 'The Basement'. We look at each other. This is confusing, why would a parcel be specifically addressed to Annabelle's basement? So if the basement has it's own address, then surely it would have its own door. We split up and start to look for the basement door. There's nothing on the outside of the house…maybe the door is accessed from the back garden? I slowly push open the back gate and it's there…the basement door.'

'I've found it, I've found the basement.'

The ladies join me in the garden and we stand and stare at the basement door. Ruth pushes her way through and immediately tries the handle. The door creaks open. Shit, now what do we do?

'Come on, let's go in.' Says Ruth with far too much enthusiasm. She's countered with caution from Teresa. 'It's private property, we can't just walk in.' 'Fuck it' replies Louisa. 'We're delivering a parcel.'

Louisa pops her head around the door before ushering us inside…'It's all clear, there's no one about.' We walk down a narrow corridor which is painted a deep red. The walls are adorned with arty black and white photographs of couples in various stages of undress…not the sort of thing I would have thought Annabelle would have gone for, but as we know she's full of surprises. We come to a door at the end of the corridor and we can hear voices. One is definitely Annabelle and the other is a male voice which sounds familiar…

'You've been a very naughty boy, haven't you?'

'I have Madam, hit me harder Madam…please.'

We don't have a fucking clue what's going on, but it sounds like a really bad porno. Ruth looks shocked and then mightily pissed off. 'I recognise that voice...the fucking fucker.' She flings open the door and we all stop dead in our tracks. The room looks like a medieval dungeon. Hanging from the walls are all manner of whips, paddles, blindfolds and handcuffs. There's a cage, what looks like a whipping bench and a swing (you don't need to know how I know what these things are). Annabelle is at the back of the room and she's wearing a black PVC catsuit. There's a man attached to a St Andrew's Cross (again, you don't need to know how I know) and she's whipping his arse. It's then that the realisation hits...Annabelle is a Dominatrix! That's her secret...she's a fucking Dominatrix! She stops when she hears the door open, but doesn't look back. She's obviously expecting somebody else;

'Just pop yourselves into the changing rooms gentlemen, I won't be too long.'

I can't believe what I'm seeing and as I'm trying to process it Ruth suddenly lets rip;

'Phillip, I know it's you. I'd recognise that scrawny arse anywhere. After everything you said to me, you're letting that evil, dried up old slapper give you a good whipping...you complete and utter fucking twat.'

Annabelle stops dead and Phillip desperately pulls at the restraints to free himself. She undoes him and I've never seen anyone move so quickly. He dives into a side room and grabs his clothes, desperately trying to put his trousers on as Ruth chases him out of the basement like a woman possessed . He's pleading with her as they leave, not to save their marriage but to make sure Ruth doesn't tell his Mother. I can't imagine the bollocking he's going to get once they are outside. I would love to be a fly on the wall when his Mother finds out what her perfect son has been up to. Annabelle doesn't seem at all phased to see us all standing there in her basement sex dungeon.

She looks triumphant, like she's won and she wants us all to know it. To think, we thought her being a secret northerner was her big secret. We would never, ever have imagined this. Never in a million years would I have thought Annabelle was a Dominatrix...she's older than my Mum! Why was she so offended by us reading Wax Whips and My Hairy Bits? It's quite tame compared to the set up she has down here. One of us needs to say something and the ladies are pushing me forward so I guess it has to be me;

'You've got a parcel Annabelle.'

You've got a parcel, fuck me. Is that best I could come out with? I don't quite know where to start and try again;

'We've been speaking to your sister Annabelle. We know you're a northerner. Why are you living a lie?'

Even that sounds a bit pathetic, but her northern roots have definitely been overshadowed by this particular revelation. She looks at me with her cold, piercing eyes and begins to speak;

'My sister is irrelevant, just another example of why I hate the north so much. She was always the gold girl, the favourite. I could never do enough to please my parents, it was always Martha this and Martha that. She was so warm and down to earth, they found her horrible flat vowels endearing…eugh, the very thought of her accent disgusts me. I couldn't compete with that and quite frankly I didn't want to, so I decided to better myself and move away. Move away from the memory of feeling second best.'

I actually start to feel a bit sorry for her. Maybe she's just misunderstood…or maybe not;

'Then you come along…typical northerner and start to threaten everything I have worked so hard for.'

I don't understand, it was a ladies book club. Why was it so important to her? As I'm pondering this we are joined by two new arrivals…George and Steven. They are chatting away as they enter the basement and don't see us until it's too late. Tara turns pale and Teresa looks like she's going to kill someone. Tara pushes past us all and gets right into George's face;

'George, how could you? How could you betray me like this. You said you were too weak, too ill to show me any attention…but you're not too weak to let Annabelle fiddle with your bits. No wondered you struggle to sit down and get up, she's been flogging your arse raw for weeks…you told me it was your heart! I felt terrible if I left you alone for five minutes. I haven't been able to live my life because I was thinking about you every waking minute of my day. Every word that comes out of your mouth is a lie. You'd make me feel guilty for putting butter on a crumpet when in reality you were stuffing your face in the pub...were you building yourself up for her? Were you even thinking about me whilst you were down here with Annabelle or were you just thinking about your dick?'

George tries to speak, but Tara is having none of it. She storms out followed by George, his apologies are falling on deaf ears...she really doesn't want to know. It's not only Tara that is pissed off...Teresa can barely contain her fury;

'You fucking piece of shit Steven...you've pushed me away, turned down my advances why? Because you'd rather be here with her than with me. Well you can fuck off mate...I'm not wasting another minute of my life on you. As for you Annabelle, what a sad little woman you are. You demanded our loyalty, when all the time you were messing about with our husbands. What kind of a human being are you?

'A successful one Teresa.'

We have to hold Teresa back, she is desperate to give Annabelle a slap and I can't say that I blame her.

'Fuck you Annabelle and fuck you Steven...get home and pack your bags.'

Teresa leaves followed by Steven who seems resigned to the fact he has royally fucked up. For the first time in his life he doesn't know what to say...what can he say? With half the group gone, there's just me, Louisa and Belinda left now. Louisa can't contain herself any longer;

'What are you playing at Annabelle? What have Tara, Ruth and Teresa ever done to you? They thought you were their friend but you've just fucking played them. I think you owe us some kind of explanation.'

'I don't owe you anything. You mean nothing to me with your sad little lives in this sad little village. Everything was working just fine until she turned up. The archetypal friendly northerner with no respect for convention. I had you all where I wanted you in my book club. Dull books, no excitement and definitely no alcohol. Then she comes along like a breath of fresh air for you all with her smutty book and her comedy. There was no way I could let it carry on and had to do everything I could to stop it. I couldn't let you find yourselves and become sexually adventurous because then your husbands wouldn't need me anymore. They came to me because you were boring, because they needed some excitement in their lives. I needed you away from her and back in my dull, tedious book club where I could keep you down. Obviously I'm only talking about Tara, Ruth and Teresa. You ladies have nothing to worry about, your husbands were tough nuts to crack and I can only congratulate you on keeping them so interested.'

So that's why she didn't want us to read the book. Annabelle was worried that if the ladies brought excitement back into their own relationships then her clients would start to dry up...what a conniving bitch. I'm not sure I feel comforted by her congratulations, she may not have been able to damage our relationships, but she's more than likely broken up three marriages.

'Don't get me wrong. I didn't have sex with any of them…I'm not that desperate. But I do enjoy dominating a weak man and if they are prepared to pay me for the privilege who am I to complain.'

'What about your husband Annabelle, what does he make of all this.'

'Quite frankly Julia, I couldn't give a shit what he thinks. We've led separate lives for so many years. He does his thing and I do mine.'

She is so cold. I don't think she feels anything for anyone.

'Anyway ladies, lovely as it was to chat to you. I'd like you to leave now. I have another client due any minute.'

Belinda has been too shocked to speak but finally finds her voice;

'Do you not feel any guilt at all Annabelle. Are you really so devoid of human emotion that you don't give a shit. These ladies regarded thought they were your friend, but you put them down and stripped them of their confidence so you could whip their husbands arses… that is seriously fucked up. I'm going to make sure everyone gets to know about this, they are going to find out what you are really like…what do you think the Vicar is going to say?'

'I don't know Belinda…why don't you ask him yourself.'

We all turn around. Annabelle's next client has arrived and it's the fucking Vicar! This just gets better and better. The Vicar! Now it becomes clear why he stopped us from using the church hall. He was doing as he was told…I don't think it's us that should be praying for God's mercy is it Vicar? He looks horrified when he realises he's been busted. He does mutter something about needing to speak to Annabelle about helping out at mass…but he can tell we're not buying it and makes a pretty sharp exit dropping his gimp mask on the way out. I do consider picking it up and returning it to him later but I get the feeling he's going to busy explaining all this to the Bishop.

'Are you still here? I thought you would have left with the Vicar. Seriously, what are you still doing here…you are really starting to irritate me.'

I try to reason with her one last time…

'This has to stop now Annabelle. You are causing too much hurt and upset.'

Louisa however is not in the mood for reasoning with anyone;

'Listen you nasty, small minded minge bucket…we don't want you here. So why don't you take your whips and your sex furniture and fuck off. Then once you've fucked off, please fuck off some more.'

I can't help but laugh at sex furniture…You've got to love Louisa. She's not sober much but when she is, she's hilarious. As we are leaving I turn and take one last look at Annabelle. She looks furious…she's finally been unmasked and I don't see where she can go from here. Who would have thought that Annabelle with her Received Pronunciation and churchly ways was actually a full on northern Dominatrix who was spanking half the men in the village.

WHAT HAPPENED NEXT?

Two months on and I'm still shocked by the events in Annabelle's basement. She really did put a bomb under village life and genuinely didn't give a shit. There's been so much change since we discovered her secret life. Within days of being caught with his pants about to come down, the Vicar moved to a different parish. It was a quick and quiet move and I'm not sure if he jumped or if he was pushed. Either way he needed to go. I for one could never have looked at him in church again without imagining him in a pair of leather shorts and a gimp mask. There was no way I would have been able to take his sermons seriously again. Can you imagine the headline if the tabloid media had got hold of the story 'Village Vicar in Dominatrix scandal.' It was story that had to be buried quickly. So we have a new Vicar, a lady...she's a fabulous, down to earth northerner. Finally I'm not the only one in the village with flat vowel sounds. I think she must have been brought fully up to speed on events in the village as the first time I met her she said she couldn't wait to join our book club and gave me a cheeky wink. I don't know if she was joking or not, but one thing I have learnt through this whole experience is book clubs and Vicars don't really mix. I suppose you want to know what happened to the ladies after that fateful day. Thankfully nothing changed for me, Belinda or Louisa but as for others? Where do I start? It's been interesting!

Ruth chased Phillip back to their house and didn't hold back with a torrent of fucks…women were covering their children's ears as she castigated him all the way home. It was such a shock for Ruth. Phillip was so straight laced, so conservative she would never have expected to see him being whipped by Annabelle in a million years…it was surreal. Ruth had supressed her personality for years to keep him happy. She didn't know any different. She had complete faith in him and then it transpires that when she thought Phillip was out train spotting he was really handcuffed to a table enjoying a bollocking from Annabelle. After her challenge had gone so horribly wrong, Ruth had almost decided that her marriage was over. The whole Annabelle episode confirmed it. When she got home with Phillip he was full of apologies, but she was having none of it. She told him to pack up the rest of his stuff and move back to his Mother's permanently. Once he had left, there was just one thing left for her to do. She phoned Phillip's Mother and told her everything. Of course she wasn't having any of it…it was Ruth's fault, she had driven him to it. In typical Ruth style she told her to 'fuck off'. Phillip has called Ruth a couple of times since he left pleading with her to take him back. Unfortunately for him, Ruth has already moved on. She's started dating Chris a gardener from the village. Their eyes met over a bush and he's been knee deep in hers ever since. Ruth is living her best life...strangely thanks to Annabelle.

Although Teresa's marriage had become a little boring over the years, she had no reason not to trust Steven. They had been together so long she had accepted that the spark they had at the beginning of their marriage had turned into a damp squib. Unfortunately for Teresa, she naively believed that if Steven was bored or stuck in a rut he would have talked to her...Annabelle got there first. She convinced him his marriage was boring and would never get better. She reeled him in and then offered her services to bring a bit of excitement back into his life. Then when Teresa found her spirit and wanted to bring some excitement into the bedroom herself, she told him that if Teresa carried on reading 'that smut' she would end up leaving him. When Teresa first saw Steven in the dungeon she was adamant her marriage was over. I don't know what he said to her when they got home, but she decided to give him one last chance. She laid down a number of rules that he had to agree to before she would agree to give their marriage a final try. He had to lose weight... if she was to get more dick, she needed to be able to see it first. He needed to stop being such a gobshite, listen to other people and accept he wasn't right all the time. Finally, he had to put her first above everything which included football, the pub and pickled eggs (which according to Teresa would repeat on him for hours). Things do seem to be going well. Teresa is much happier and Steven certainly looks like he is starting to lose weight. I hope that despite Annabelle's interference they can come back stronger than ever.

It was Tara that worried me the most. As much as George was dependant on her, she seemed dependant on him. George was her whole world and looking after him was her way of life. I couldn't have been more wrong. The minute they got home she started throwing his belongings out of the bedroom window…'Take your fucking clothes and fuck off George, maybe you can get Annabelle to do the packing for you. Oh no I forgot Annabelle just spanks your arse, it's me that's had to wipe it all these years'…it caused quite a crowd to gather. I don't think the village had been that entertained in years. I almost felt sorry for George as he was scrabbling amongst the holly bushes to pick up his belongings. The minute Tara saw George in the basement the scales fell away from her eyes. She realised that he had basically been taking the piss out of her. Tara thought he was ill and he used that his advantage…he had her catering to his every whim. When in reality he was perfectly fine, using his 'walks' as a cover for visiting Annabelle. There was no coming back from this betrayal for Tara and no amount of apologies were going to change her mind. George left and she hasn't mentioned him since. She's started divorce proceedings and just wants to get on with the rest of her life. Tara is now on Tinder and delights in showing us the regular dick pics she receives…she's come alive and it's so good to see.

So what happened to Annabelle. A couple of days after we had discovered her secret a removal van pulled up outside her house. Annabelle was nowhere to be seen and the removal men only seemed to clearing out the basement. Things got stranger still when later no that day there was a knock on my door and you imagine the look on my face when I opened it to be greeted by Annabelle;

'Hello Julia, I'm sure you're wondering what I'm doing here.'

I was completely flabbergasted, what was she doing on my doorstep?

'I wanted to explain myself. I accept that my behaviour may have caused distress to some of the ladies in the village. I accept that I have used and manipulated certain villagers for my own benefit and I finally accept that I should never have denied my northern roots. Am I sorry? Not particularly…I'm sure you're shocked to hear that Julia, but I have absolutely no regrets. I moved to this village thirty years ago, married Giles and had two children…children who grew up, left home and want nothing to do with me.'

The word 'karma' suddenly springs to mind.

'I was bored, everyday is the same in this village. Giles had his bit on the side so he didn't give a shit what I did…and yes it did hurt in the beginning but I wasn't going anywhere until he got his pension. There was no way I was going to let that cheap tart interfere with my divorce settlement. We lived separate lives. I didn't ask any questions and neither did he. The basement came about after I watched a documentary about a Dominatrix...I found it fascinating and saw so much of myself in the woman they were following. I got the builders in to work on my basement the very next day. I targeted the men I thought were most bored in their marriages and I enjoyed every minute of it. I didn't need to have sex with any of these men, but I could dominate them...I finally had full control. That was until you turned up. You reminded me of my past, of everything I left behind and I hated you for it. I hated you even more for introducing the ladies to that book. I could see everything I had built up slipping away from me and I admit I behaved terribly. I can't stay here, that's quite clear and now Giles finally has his rather large pension it seems like a good time for me to leave. As soon as you all left the basement I made a call to my sister and after all these years we have reconciled. So I'm moving home...back up north. Martha lives alone in our parents old house. It has a huge basement and we've decided to go into business together...imagine all those stag parties and holiday makers looking for a bit of fun. I've already started thinking about merchandise...'Whip me quick' hats and sticks of rock...I could make a fortune. Maybe I've been to harsh on the north...this could be the best thing that's happened to me in a long time. I really didn't mean any harm to the ladies. I genuinely thought I was doing them a favour...the state of their husbands I can fully understand why they wouldn't want to go there. Anyway Julia I can't say it's been a pleasure meeting you, but I wish you the best.'

...and with that she was gone. I don't think I'll ever meet anyone like Annabelle again and I really don't want to. I was surprised that Annabelle's sister was so forgiving...she must be a good, decent human being, what a shame she's now stuck with the bitch troll sister from hell. Her loss is our gain and I have nothing but sympathy for every poor northerner that is going to be exposed to Annabelle's bullshit. Now she's gone, we can all move on with our lives...in peace and harmony. There's going to be no more book club meetings, we've become such good friends we meet up at least once a week anyway and there's always plenty of prosecco and cake on offer. We've all been seeing much more of Giles since Annabelle left. I think he feels more comfortable and less embarrassed facing people now that she's gone. He's such a nice man...you would never have them put them together. He hasn't told us much about his marriage to Annabelle, but apparently she told him it was over years ago. He only started seeing someone else when he was convinced his relationship couldn't be saved...he must have been a very patient man to try and work through things through with that woman. After she left he introduced us to his girlfriend Felicity and she is absolutely lovely... couldn't be more different to Annabelle and I'm so pleased she's joining us all at Louisa's next week so we can fill her in on all the gossip.

It was a shame we didn't get around to my challenge on the reveal night, I had so much to tell them. So just in case you were wondering, my challenge was to drip hot wax all over my husband…how did I get on? Well, I'm pleased to say I more than succeeded in my challenge. The hot wax went down so well we decided to complete the rest of the list…what would Annabelle say?

Thank you for reading and I hope you enjoyed 'Secrets, Lies and The Book Club Wives'. If you were wondering if the book mentioned in the story. 'Wax, Whips and My Hairy Bits' actually exists...well, it does and I know it does because I wrote it! It's available to buy now and to follow is the book blurb and the first chapter.

WAX WHIPS AND MY HAIRY BITS

Ann has spent a lifetime reading safe, charming romantic novels leading to a series of dull, unexciting relationships where the sex has been uninspiring and her needs and desires have come second place to a quick shag and a pint of Guinness. After experiencing an awakening she decides things have to change and she embarks on an erotic adventure. Join her in her quest for sexual liberation as she unleashes the passion within her and goes on a journey to discover her very own Mr. Uninhibited.

You'll be rooting for Ann as her desire to emulate the erotica she has read develops into a comedy of erotic errors. From hair remover cream to handcuffs, nothing turns out as she hopes and she soon begins to realise that not everything or everyone is as they seem. Ann appears to be on an never ending learning curve but will she actually learn anything or is she destined for erotic mediocrity?

CHAPTER ONE

Me

I used to love reading romance novels, nothing modern, just good old fashioned Victorian romantic literature. It was a time of innocence, the pace of life was slower, the men more charming. A time where you didn't have to conform to female stereotypes online, where you never needed to ask 'does my arse look big in this' because everyone looked big in a bustle and no fucker was going to get a look at your arse until you had a ring on your finger. It gave me hope that there was a Mr Romance out there for us all and then suddenly it dawned on me that actually it was all a little bit dull. It took me a bit of time to realise where it was all going wrong, but then it became clear. These novels, lovely as they were, were missing one vital component…they didn't do cock.

My name is Ann, not regal Anne, just plain, boring, unexciting Ann. I often wonder how my life would have turned out if my parents had just given me that extra 'e'. I am thirty-two years old, no spring chicken and no stranger to the dating scene. I work in marketing which isn't as glamorous as it sounds and if I'm honest it bores the shit out of me. The search for my Mr Romance had led me to a succession of short, infuriating relationships where the sex had been no more exciting than a blow job and a quick shag (missionary position).

I needed less Mr Romance and more Mr Uninhibited. I needed excitement, hot wax and a fucking good seeing to. I was single, more than ready to mingle and had read a shit load of Erotica so I knew exactly what I had to do in order to embark on a new sexual adventure. I wanted no strings sex, none of that emotional bollocks, just a good hard fuck and maybe a cup of coffee in the morning. I'm bored of feeling boring. I don't want to be Ann who's a good laugh, I want to be Ann who's amazing in bed, I want to be the shag that stays with you a lifetime, never bettered or forgotten.

My longest relationship had lasted nearly two years, Hayden. We met when we were both at university. I was so young and inexperienced I didn't really know what a good shag was. I lost my virginity to him after four bottles of Diamond White and maybe it was because I was pissed, or maybe because he was shit at shagging, but it was a completely underwhelming experience. There was no earth shaking orgasm, just the feeling something was missing and a sore fanny for a couple of days. We muddled along, foreplay was always the same, I gave him a blow job, he tried to find my clitoris...the man needed a fucking map. Sex was nearly always missionary, I'd sneak on top whenever I could, but he'd always flip me over for a quick finish. Maybe we just became too familiar with each other but when he started to not take his socks off when we had a shag I knew it was time to move on. He wasn't that arsed to be honest, I think he'd started to prefer his games console to me anyway and if he could have stuck his knob in it I'm sure he would have dumped me before I dumped him. My relationship history since Hayden has been unremarkable, hence my decision to ditch the romance novels and dive head long, or should that be muff long, into Erotica.

I'm suppose you could say I'm reasonably pretty and my face is holding up well, which is surprising given my twenty a day smoking habit, absolute love of kebabs and a probable dependency on Prosecco. My tits aren't too bad, they measure in at a 36C and I'm pleased to say they are still nice and perky and probably a few years off resembling a Spaniel's ears. My legs are long and shapely and the cellulite on my arse can be hidden with a good, supportive pair of knickers. Thongs just aren't going to happen, sorry Erotica but negotiating with a piece of cheese wire up my arse does not do it for me whatsoever. I've been researching my subject well recently, and one of the first rules when embarking on an erotic adventure seems to be that one must have a shaven haven, a freshly mown lawn, a smooth muff...I think you get the picture. I need to think carefully about how I am going to achieve my erotica ready fanny as the expression 'bearded clam' doesn't describe the half of it!

I don't fancy having my fanny flaps waxed and shaving isn't really an option as I'm petrified I'll get a shaving rash. So the only option I've got is hair remover cream. A quick trip to the shops and it's mission accomplished; my lady garden is smothered in intimate hair remover cream. It looks like a Mr Whippy with sprinkles but definitely no chocolate flake. It's not the most attractive look in the world, I'm staggering around like a saddle sore old cowboy, but it's going to be worth it…I am Ann without an 'e' and without pubes, a bald fannied paragon of sexual liberation. That bird with the posh name in 50 shades of whatever is going to have nothing on me! Though I have to admit, the undercarriage was a bit of a nightmare and to be honest it does sting a bit. At least I don't have to wait too long and then I will be smooth, shiny and….ouch…I'm fucking burning now! Burning is not right surely? Jesus, my flaps are on fire. Give me a minute I need to jump in the shower and get this shit off.

I just spent four fucking hours in A&E. I washed the cream off and my minge was glowing red and burning like a bastard which was almost bearable until the swelling started. I could feel my lips starting to throb, they were pulsating like a rare steak. I didn't want to look down, but I knew I had to…fuck me I had testicles, just call me Johnny Big Bollocks because that is what I had. I quickly checked Dr Google and the best thing for swelling is elevation and an ice pack, so I spent the best part of half an hour with my minge in the air and a packet of frozen peas clamped between my thighs. Needless to say it had no effect at all and it became painfully clear that I was going to have to haul my now damp, swollen crotch to the hospital. Never before have I felt so humiliated, having to describe in intimate detail my problem to little Miss Smug Bitch at reception;

'So, you've come to A&E today because your vagina is swollen'…

...well it's my vulva actually but let's not split pubic hairs, or try and get them off with cunting hair remover cream. Sour face huffed and puffed and eventually booked me in, I spent what felt like an eternity pacing around...I couldn't sit down, my testicles wouldn't allow it and by this time a ball bra wouldn't have gone amiss. The Doctor I saw, who was absolutely gorgeous (the one time I didn't want to show an attractive man my fanny) and, when he wasn't stifling a laugh, couldn't have been more sympathetic. I'd had an allergic reaction and he'd prescribe me some anti-histamines which would bring the swelling down, my labia would return to their normal size and other than some skin sensitivity for a few days I would be fine but under no circumstances was I to use hair remover cream again as next time the reaction could be even worse. Though what could be worse than the whopping set of bollocks I'd grown I don't know. So that's that, I'm going to have to go au natural. Which is fine by me, I'd rather have a hairy beaver than an angry one.

A few hours later and my muff has more or less returned to normal and other than feeling slightly itchy seems to be perfectly fine. I've crossed shaven haven off my to do list and need to carry on with my preparation. As you may have already gathered, I've got a lot of work to do. I've noticed in most of the Erotica I've read that the words penis and vagina are rarely used, so I need to practise my sexual vocabulary, I need to learn how to talk dirty...I need to do my Erotica homework. I've had another flick through some of my books and there's no way I can call my vagina 'my sex' I know strictly speaking it is, but for fuck's sake…'my sex craves you', 'my sex needs your sex' it's all sounds a bit contrived if you ask me so I think I'll check out the Urban Dictionary.

I've just spent a good hour trawling through and my God what an education that was. Either I'm more wet behind the ears than I thought I was or some of the things I've just read are made up, check out 'Angry Pirate'…that's not for real, is it? I'm ready to try some of the new words and phrases I've learnt. I need to be all pouty lipped and doe eyed as I look in the mirror, moisten my lips and purr:

'I want to suck your length'

'Do you want to drink out of my cream bucket'

'My clit is hard and ready to be licked'

'My vagina is the most magical place in the world, come inside'

What the fuck was I thinking, I can't say this shit! Firstly the doe eyed, pouty lip thing makes me look like I'm pissed and secondly I can't do this without laughing. I'm much more comfortable with 'do you fancy a pint of Guinness and a quick shag'. I quickly give my head a wobble, comfortable is boring. I'm in this for the excitement and the clit tingling thrill (see I did learn something). Maybe I'll just opt for quiet and mysterious, let my body do the talking and my mouth do the sucking (I'm really starting to get this now). So that's the plan, my persona will be a sultry erotic goddess who doesn't say much, I'll be irresistible, a fabulous shag who doesn't want a conversation, no chat just sex.

The last part of my preparation is what on earth am I going to wear? If I'm going for the mysterious look does that mean I'm going to have to channel my inner sex goddess, or does it mean I go for a prim and proper, hair up, professional look? Maybe a combination of both, tight fitting dress, hair up and glasses, then I can do the whole taking my glasses off and flicking my hair down thing. The hair flicking thing however is a bit of an issue for me: my hair is naturally curly...really curly, at university my nickname was 'pube head' which probably tells you all you need to know, so I'm going to have to straighten it to within an inch of its life. From frump to fox...check me out. Today is going to be an exciting day. I'm just waiting for the postman to arrive, I've ordered some proper lingerie. I've gone for two sets initially, traditional black and racy red. Shit, should I have ordered a dildo? I forgot about a fucking dildo and candles, I forgot candles! What about a butt plug... what actually is a butt plug? I can't be erotic if I'm not dripping hot wax on him whilst pleasuring myself with a multi speed vibrating dildo...okay, so maybe not at the same time but you get my drift. Handcuffs! Shit, I'm not very good at this, he'll just have to tie me up with my big knickers.

The postman came, and I swear he had a knowing glint in his eye when he asked me to sign for my delivery or maybe he just read the label on the back of the parcel, cheeky bastard. It took me a while to build up the courage but here I am, standing in front of a full length mirror wearing a bright red, lacy push up bra, matching arse covering comfortable pants, a suspender belt and black stockings. I'm not sure. My tits are standing to attention and look like boiled eggs in a frilly egg cup, they are virtually dangling from my ear lobes and I swear you can see my minge stubble. So the new plan will be to go for subdued or even better, no lighting at all. I think it's all starting to look really erotic… bushy fanny, no filthy talking and everything done in the dark. The scene is set and I'm ready to get out there. No strings, erotic sex here I come. Well, not quite, I need to sign up to a dating site.

I take a selfie of myself looking as sultry as possible (not doe eyed or pouty, we know that doesn't work) I decide to show a little bit of cleavage and a little bit of leg, but not too much I want to leave my potential dates gagging to see more…I'm such a temptress. I've written and rewritten my profile about twenty times, it has to be just right and I think on my twenty first attempt I've finally done it:

'Flirty thirty two year old,

I work in marketing,

I like to get my head down in both the boardroom and the bedroom,

I'm looking for no strings attached fun,

Hobbies include reading, cooking and amateur dramatics.'

I know, you don't have to tell me, it's painfully shit. Hopefully they'll just look at my profile picture and to be honest at this point I don't care, I've submitted everything and I am now a fully paid up member of a dating site.

It takes a couple of hours for my phone to eventually ping with a notification that I have a message, I'm trembling with excitement as I open it…

'You've got nice tits'

Fuck me, 'You've got nice tits' is that it? I mean it's nice he thinks I've got nice tits, but I was expecting a little bit more. No, hang on he's sent a picture…it's a dick! He's sent me a picture of his dick, eww I don't think I've ever seen such a stumpy little penis, it's got a hugely bulbous bellend which looks like it's going to explode at any minute and hang on, it looks like it's winking at me…I'm never going to be able to unsee that! I quickly delete the message, when my phone pings again…It's another dick, not the same dick, this one is long, thin and veiny as fuck. Maybe I'm being too fussy, knobs aren't supposed to be attractive are they? My phone is quickly becoming a rogues gallery of ugly shlongs. I'm really starting to think maybe this wasn't a good idea, I know I said I wanted plenty of cock, but this wasn't exactly what I meant. Three cocks later and just as I am about to give up on the whole idea (maybe a pint of Guinness and a quick shag isn't too bad after all) I get a message from Daniel. I check out his profile and he actually looks quite fit, he's good looking, athletic and he didn't send me a dick pic.

I've been chatting to Daniel over the past few days and I have to admit he sounds lovely, we seem to have quite a bit in common but I can't get carried away by our shared love of ABBA. I'm after a filthy, lustful shag, nothing more nothing less. I'm happy for him to make me come and then go. Next time he calls, I'm going to ask if he fancies going on a date, wish me luck!

Yes! He actually said yes, I am officially going on a date. Once it actually sinks in that I have a date, I start to panic. What am I going to wear, where are we going to go, will I be able to straighten my hair enough to flick it flirtatiously, how much muff stubble am I going to have?

'Wax, Whips and My Hairy Bits' is available to buy now!

And...while I still have you here I'd like to recommend another book of mine 'Fakes, Freaks, Cheats Liars & Celebrities' - it's an outrageous thriller set in the world of celebrity that is by turns very funny, shockingly outrageous and very, very dark...here's the book blurb and some sample chapters...

Fakes, Freaks, Cheats, Liars & Celebrities

Fame. Lies. Scandal. Drugs. Sex. **MURDER**.
 Celebrities have secrets to die for.

Andrew Manning has spent 20 years saving celebrities from the consequences of their own bad behavior and is known in the business as' The King of Scandal'. But now some particularly difficult and demanding characters are about strain even his legendary abilities:

Shelley, model and fashion icon, who's determined not just to blackmail her equally famous husband but also to destroy him.

Joey, an insecure reality TV star, desperate to hang on to his celebrity, even if it means slowly poisoning himself to death.

The Producer, a king in the world of entertainment and a serial abuser of hopeful young wannabe's. But this time he's picked the wrong girl for his perverted pleasures.

Charlie, morbidly obese, murderous mafiosi adviser to...

Janey, pop music goddess, a celebrity with peculiarly sharp teeth and disturbing eating habits that are about to be revealed to the public by an ambitious young paparazzo.

And then there's Johnny, Andrew's partner, a psychopath with a heart of gold who's on a mission to murder as many celebrities as possible.

Will Andrew be able to reconcile the demands of so

many different and desperate characters, and who's going to end up dead?

'Fakes, Freaks, Cheats Liars & Celebrities' - four sample chapters

Please find to follow four sample chapters taken, more or less, from the beginning, middle and end of the book...

In this first extract we meet Janey, international superstar; mad, bad, dangerous to know and possibly a vampire...

JANEY. MAKING AN ENTRANCE

As the limo speeds away from Heathrow, Janey is delighted with the way things went. What an entrance! The moment she stepped into the arrivals lounge it had been total chaos: screaming fans, paparazzi, cameramen, microphones, journalists, police, security. All there for her, Janey Jax. She is a *star*. No one comes close to her. Rivals come, rivals go and still she stays at the top, numero uno. Untouchable. Look at that Missy Go Go. Where is she now? Nowhere. Skank.

Of course, she could have flown over in the private jet, but with a world tour about to kick off and a new album coming up she needed an entrance with maximum impact, at least that's what Charlie had advised and, as always, Charlie had been right.

The day's events have left her tired, though. So tired.

People forget that she's not a young girl anymore. She may still look like she's in her twenties but, in reality, she's far removed from that happy decade. Nowadays, it takes hard work to keep looking as good as she does. Hard work and fresh, young flesh. Very young flesh. She hopes Charlie won't have any problems sourcing what she needs here in England. But, no, she shouldn't worry, Charlie is very capable. He knows what she wants, and he is bound to her. By blood. He is her creature.

In this second extract we meet foul-mouthed, homophobic Shelley. Shelley wants Andrew to blackmail her famous, gay husband into giving her a huge divorce settlement, but Shelley has her own dark secret...

SHELLEY. TIME FOR A QUICK SMOKE?

Finally, the slow and tedious drive through London's crawling traffic is over and Shelley arrives at Anthea's house in Holland Park, she always stays there when she's in London. She and Anthea are Best Friends Forever. They've known each other since way back, from when they were in "Girls Gone Wild." There were four girls in the (quite successful at the time) band but Shelley only ever really liked Anthea. Chardonnay and Alicia were bitches and cunts, and where they fuck are they now? Losers! They hadn't been smart, but Anthea and Shelley had been. Shelley had used the band as a base from which to start her solo career, Anthea had exploited her celebrity and good looks to grab herself an extremely ugly but ridiculously rich banker. Christ, Shelley can feel nothing but admiration for the way she played that prick! Led him by the fucking nose, married him, stuck with him for a couple of years, then divorced him, taking almost everything he had. Honestly, men can be such gullible dickheads, show them a bit of tit and a glimpse of snatch and, in no time at all, you can have them behaving like well-trained dogs!

Once inside Anthea's house (she has her own key, that's how BFF she and Anthea are), she makes straight for the beautiful living room and throws herself into a gorgeous sofa, dropping her Prada bag onto a gorgeous coffee table, which rests on a gorgeous carpet. Shelley *really* likes Anthea's place, she makes her mind up that she too will buy a home in Holland Park when the divorce money comes through from Jack faggotpants.

Yes, the divorce settlement, more money, more success…what a wonderful day it's been! It's going to be so great when Anthea gets back from her latest shopping trip. Shelley can't wait to tell her what's about to happen to Jack, how she's about to blackmail him into a *huge* pay out. Hah, she is *so* going to screw him! Nobody fucks with Shelley!

Shelley muses happily for some minutes about her upcoming freedom from Jack and her fabulous future career in America, until her thoughts stray, unstoppably, to that package, nestled comfortably in the Prada bag. She takes it out, rolls it around in her hands, a greedy and needing expression on her face. Using her sharp finger nails, she quickly tears at and then unwraps the cellophane from the package, to reveal a substantial, round rock of crack cocaine. She places the rock of crack on Anthea's gorgeous coffee table. Taking a nail file from her handbag she begins to chip away at the off-white coloured lump, which has a texture somewhere between wax and brittle plastic. Expertly she detaches smaller rocks from the main block, each new rock just the right size for a single good hit when smoked. There's loads of crack here, enough to last her and Anthea a couple of nights, if they don't go too mad! As well as BFFs, she and Anthea are also BDBs, Best Drug Buddies.

She loves her crack does Shelley, fantastic stuff. Okay, so maybe the next day you might feel a bit down, a bit paranoid, but nothing that can't be smoothed out with a few drinks. Or some more crack. And the hit, Christ the hit! Once felt never forgotten! She knows of course that she shouldn't really be smoking it, what with her being famous, rich and beautiful and in a responsible position due to her influence over the young people of the world, but the public just doesn't realise that being famous, rich and beautiful is very hard work. Every day is filled with questions. What should I wear? Am I slim enough? How's my make-up today? Have I got the right handbag for this or that occasion? Who should I be *seen* to be speaking to? Which party do I go to, and which should I snub? Where should I be this afternoon to stand the best chance of being papped? These are all difficult and complex questions. Being a celeb is a demanding business, not everybody can handle it. Her lifestyle involves a lot of a pressure, and the crack is Shelley's way of relaxing, of dealing with the stress she endures every day. She deserves it. She is *entitled* to it.

Of course she has been in trouble with the crack before, resulting in some fairly unpleasant media coverage, but she had dealt with that, although it did involve some help from that hideous queer, Andrew. But that's all in the past. She's much more careful now, more discreet, she'll never be caught again. "Never say never," says a little voice somewhere in the back of Shelley's head, but she chooses to ignore it.

Shelley wonders if she should smoke a quick rock before

Anthea gets back? Why the hell not!

In this third extract we meet Joey, a handsome young reality TV star. Joey's career has gone into free fall after launching an expletive laden attack against the Queen of England on live TV. In an effort to save Joey's career, Andrew prescribes a convenient case of pretend 'celebrity cancer' but Joey has a plan of his own...

JOEY. "I LOVE THE VERY BONES OF YOU"

Joey is woken early that morning by the Philipina nurse, fussing around. Making sure all his wires and tubes are in the proper place, he presumes. Actually, is "woken" the right word? Does he really fall asleep and wake up nowadays, or does he just drift in and out of consciousness? Joey's not sure but he thinks probably the latter.

Yesterday was a big day for Joey, he's surprised that he got through it. Saying goodbye to his kids, Christ that was hard. He'd had pretty much a repeat conversation with his ma and da later on. He told them that he felt that he didn't have long left (a message that Joey knew Andy's dodgy doctor would reinforce to them). His mum kept saying "don't be silly, Joey lad, you'll get through this," but he could see from her eyes that she didn't believe it, and she could see from his that he didn't believe it either.

As he explained his (recently made up) philosophy of time as great circle, with spirits racing around it and meeting again and again as different people, but always instinctively recognising each other, well, he could see it seemed odd to his parents. At times they looked at him as though he was delirious, but he got over his central message to them. Then he explained that the twins would be their responsibility, that there was plenty of money coming their way after he died and, most of all, that he loved them dearly and he was grateful beyond words for everything they had ever done for him, that he was immensely proud that they were his parents. He wonders what they'd think should they ever find out the reason for his illness, not cancer, but his own self-administered poison. They must never know that. Joey is grateful that only Andy knows the full story behind his condition. His secrets are safe with Andy.

Having checked all his various tubes and wires, the nurse helps Joey, on his request, to move position in his bed, from lain flat to sitting up. Joey has very little strength and the poor girl has to push and pull mostly on her own. Joey's grateful that, though only a small woman, she seems to have surprising strength. Together, they get him into a sitting up in bed position. The nurse plumps up pillows behind his back, puts one behind his head. She asks him if he needs anything else, does he need the bedpan? No thanks (there's nothing in him to shit out), but could she open the curtains and maybe get him a small glass of water? Thank you.

The nurse opens the curtains, and daylight streams in. Joey thinks it must be a beautiful day outside. The realisation hits him like a physical blow. Shit. This is it. It's a beautiful day and it's this day that I'll leave this world. Today is the day I die. I'll not see any more beautiful days. I'll not see any more days, full stop. Joey is hit with a huge sense of loss. You know what, despite all the shit, all the grief and all the idiots and haters it really is a beautiful, beautiful world. His thoughts are interrupted as the nurse returns with his water. She holds the glass to his lips and helps him take a few small sips. He asks her to leave the glass by his bed.

Joey slips back into sleep/unconsciousness, he dreams. He dreams a gorgeous dream. If his dream were a film it would be in widescreen, Technicolor, 3D, high definition, the whole shooting match. He dreams he is with the twins, his ma and da are there, and Andy and three of his oldest friends from his Doncaster days: Liz, Helen and Susan. They're all at Blackpool Pleasure Beach. There's nobody else there, it's empty, fantastic, the whole thing open just for them! And Joey's body is well again, it's young, healthy, vital, it is whole.

In the dream everybody is having a great time, they eat candyfloss and donuts, the twins go mad in the arcades, piling a stream of coins, that just keep spewing from the machines like magic, into the slotties and video games. Then they hit the rides. There are no queues, nothing to pay, they just walk on. They do the Dodgems, laughing hysterically as they bump into each other, they enjoy twirling on the Teacups ride, whizzing through the air in the old Hiram Maxim flying machines, thrilled as they take a ride through time in the River Caves, pretend to get scared on the ghost train. Then after more donuts and candyfloss it's time for the grand finale: the Big Dipper. They all squeeze close up together in one giant dream-sized Big Dipper car and they're off, racing along the track. Normally Joey hates this kind of thing, but this dream Big Dipper is special. It's fast but smooth and, surrounded by such happy friends and family, Joey feels totally safe and secure. The Dipper speeds along, slows as it whizzes round a sharp bend, and then begins to climb a hill that seems to go on forever. It soars high up above the Pleasure Beach, then up above Blackpool, and looking to his left and right Joey can see way beyond the town and far out to sea. All the other rides become small, toy town in size and now the hill is so high that the view is like that from a plane. Joey is aware that the Dipper is pushing up higher and higher into the sky and he looks down and beneath him he can see big, fluffy pink clouds, like the candyfloss he has just eaten. Then huge objects appear above Joey's head: vast, snowflake-like constructions made of sparkling, clear ice, desperately beautiful and delicate and filled with a brilliant and warming, white inner light and Joey knows that they are stars. He is amazed, fascinated. They are so beautiful that they move him almost to tears. Then, as if it had decided it could go no further up, the Big Dipper car begins to descend, travelling down a huge and straight slope that seems to go on and on and on. It charges down, faster and faster, the wind whistles through Joey's hair, he feels an exhilarating freedom, everyone is loving it, Joey is loving it. But then he feels himself detach from the car, sucked out by the wind caused by its downward plunge. He's not scared, though, not worried. This sudden detachment seems like the most natural thing in the world. He flaps his arms and, just he as knew would happen, he can fly. He flies after the Dipper car for a while, but he can't keep up with its breakneck speed and he sees his family and friends are waving back at him from the car and shouting. They are smiling, they are saying "goodbye, Joey, we love you." Joey calls after them "I love you too," and stops trying to follow. He knows where he must go now, and feeling light and happy he begins to fly upward, back up to those beautiful, snowflake shaped stars.

Suddenly, Joey's dream vanishes. He is awake, disturbed by some bizarre burning pain in his chest. He's pissed off, that was a lovely dream. If only he could have stayed there! The ever present nurse has seen him stirring and ask if he's alright, "I'm fine, love," he says but grimaces in pain, the nurse notices and asks if he would like morphine. He thinks about accepting, but this is his last day, he doesn't want to spend any more of it asleep or in that warm morphine haze, so he answers in the negative and asks the nurse if she has the time and she replies, "it's just gone three o'clock , sir"

"Please, don't call me "sir" anymore, it's Joey, and you, what's your name?"

"Amor, sir...Joey."

"Amor, that's a lovely name. Amor, I want to thank you for all the 'elp you've given me, you're a great nurse an" you 'ave a very sweet nature"

Amor beams from ear to ear and says "thank you, Joey, you're a kind man, a good man."

"Now then, enough of all this compliment swapping," says Joey trying to set a light tone, "'elp me sit back up will you?"

After some mutual huffing, puffing, pulling and pushing, Joey is back in a more upright position. Shit, he thinks, Andy will be here anytime now. He checks the glass of water is still

by his bed. Yes, it is, good. So this it. The end. He has less than an hour to live. God! He's not scared though, that dream he had has been strangely reassuring. He's ready to go, happy to go, to be honest, glad to escape the pain and discomfit that's been the main feature of his life for so long now. Sorry to leave everyone, of course, but, following his new philosophy of life and death, hopeful that it won't be for ever. Joey is about as prepared to die as any man can be.

There's a quiet knock at his bedroom door. Slowly it opens and first one head pops round, then another and another. Amazing! It's just like his bloody dream! It's Liz, Helen and Sue. "My girls!" cries Joey in delight, "come in, come in, it's so good to see you!"

The girls move as one, they come to Joey in his bed, Liz sits one side, Helen and Sue sit on the other. They're all touches and greetings, kissing Joey's cheeks, holding his hands, running their hands through his once thick hair. "Your mam called us last night, Joey," says Sue, "she told us you'd love to see us and so here we are."

"You mean," says Joey "that she told you you'd best get down 'ere quick like, before I go."

"Well, she said you weren't good, but you're going to pull through this, Joey," says Liz.

"Liz, girls, its good of you to say that but truth is I'm dyin', but I'm ready, I don't want no tears or sympathy so you three pull ya selves together...anyway, tell me, you musta left Doncaster bloody early to get 'ere for now, how's things up there, then?"

And so it goes, Joey spends a delightful forty minutes chatting away to his three old friends. He's always loved these girls, they were his best friends at school (he never really got on with other boys, he can see now that that wasn't a failing on his part, he just pissed them off because he was too bloody good-looking). They remained friends after school, and when Joey became famous, they were always there for him, a shoulder to cry on when things were bad, a source of mostly good advice and someone to share his success with. They were never envious of that success, never asked for more than he could give, they were always true friends.

And then, sadly, this sweet little chat has to end, Andy has arrived. He's standing in the open door of Joey's bed room, looks very smart, thinks Joey. He likes Andy's suit, Armani he guesses. Joey waves Andy forward, saying, "Andy, come in, these are friends of mine from Doncaster, Liz, Helen and Sue, girls, this is Andy. 'e's a friend an' 'e kinda 'elps me out wi' me, er, legal stuff." Andy and the girls exchange handshakes and greetings, Joey can tell that Andy's a bit stressed and seems a bit hurried, he's moving a bit funny too, like somebody had kicked him in the balls. Joey senses Andy needs his attention so he says, "girls, Amor, can me an' Andy 'ave bit of privacy for a few minutes? There's some stuff I'ave to talk about wi' 'im, business, that sorta nonsense." Of course, nod the girls and the nurse and they make their way out of his room, Andy following and closing the door behind them.

"Joey," says Andy looking nervous, rubbing his hands together and smiling rather fixedly as he does so, "how are you and are you ready for this? Christ, sorry, that's a stupid question, I…I just don't really know what to say, I've never helped anyone top themselves before!"

"That's okay, Andy, it's fine, don't worry, I ain't never topped meself before so I don't know what to say either!"

"And you're sure that this is what you want, that this is what you really, really want?"

"Absolutely sure, I'm exhausted, I just can't fight to keep meself alive anymore…just one thing, though…it won't 'urt will it, Andy…?"

In this fourth extract we meet Carrie. Carrie works for Andrew but harbours her own secret desire for celebrity. We join Carrie after she's had a bruising encounter with the sexually abusive entertainment mogul, The Producer. Ashamed and angry with herself for being so naïve, Carrie wonders what on earth she should do...until she encounters an Angel in a coffee-shop who has some good advice for her...

CARRIE'S STORY

After running out of *that* man's office, Carrie fled deeper into the anonymity of Soho, seeking shelter and safety in aloneness. She sits now in one of those soulless chain coffee shops, on her own, seat by the window, hunched over a large mug of the brown, bland muck that passes for coffee in these places, steaming like a warm cup of piss on the table in front of her.

She is appalled with herself. She is jittery. She is shaking with shame and anger. How could she have been so utterly stupid as to have her own secret dreams of stardom when she works in the world of celebrity? She knows, better than most, that it is a world of fakes and freaks, trickery, lies, abusers and cheats. But no, despite that fact, despite the fact that she's got a great, well-paid, interesting job and has lovely workmates, despite all that she has her secret, stupid bloody dream of being a singer.

And because of that, she ends up in that office. With that man. That pig. Dirty, disgusting, pig. Invited in to "discuss her career." For goodness sake, how stupidly naïve. She should have known something was wrong when he started going on about how she was older than his usual type of girl, but so pretty and so fresh-faced and reached under his desk and pressed something that closed the door and blinds of his office. Then he started coming out with all that crap about trust and commitment and he asked her to take her top off. When she wouldn't do it the dirty old git became abusive, stood up, came up to her, put his face in hers, mouthing obscenities and stuck his hand between her legs.

That was her more than enough for Carrie. She kneed the scumbag in the balls. Hard. He fell to the floor, huffing and puffing in pain, and she aimed a quick kick to his face and was pleased to hear a satisfying crunch as his nose broke under the impact of her foot. From there she was right on her toes, round the back of the guy's desk, found the cheeky little button he'd pressed to lock the office door, pushed it, door opens, she jumps over the prostate figure of the revolting piece of filth and she's out of the office and out of the building.

Christ. What does she do now? She wants to punish the dirty, nasty pig: a knee in the balls and a busted nose isn't enough. She wants to screw him over, see him broken, destroyed, maybe even dead, not just for her but for all the other people that she is absolutely sure he's done this to before. But how? She knows the way fame and wealth work, knows there is no point going to the Old Bill or the media. Like that'll get her anywhere, this guy is far too rich and influential to be troubled by minor nonsense like police and press.

What on earth is she going to do? She needs to talk

to someone about this, if not to get revenge then at least for her own sanity. Carrie pauses in her thoughts and stares down at her rapidly cooling mug of coffee-type drink. She looks up, and catches sight of an old tramp shuffling around the coffee bar, he's going from table to table, asking for money, getting nothing but refusals in the form of stunted shrugs and a half-mumbled "no, no." The tramp looks up from his latest unsuccessful prospect and his and Carrie's eyes meet. He is a ragged, dirty, rumpled man but, God, the eyes! To Carrie his eyes burn with an incredible intensity of intelligence and compassion. They are spellbinding. She can't understand why no one else has noticed them, why they should dismiss so readily a man who so obviously shines from his soul. The tramp smiles at Carrie, looking at her as though she's the exact person he's just popped into the coffee shop to meet. He heads straight for her table and in seconds, he is standing by her. He smells bad, of sweat and dirty clothes, but Carrie hardly notices, she is entranced by those eyes, waves of understanding and love seem to flow from them and she feels warm and comforted, as if someone has woven a net beneath her to catch her should she fall. She is convinced that she is in the company of an angel. A dirty, smelly, ragged angel, but an angel nevertheless. The tramp/angel opens his mouth and says to her to tell Johnny, Johnny will know what to do. Johnny will make everything right. And with that he turns away, walks out of the coffee bar and vanishes instantly into the crowds of Soho.

As if he had never been there.

Carrie is confused. She's calm and happy, her strange visitor has definitely improved her mood, but she's confused. Why did she think that the tramp was angel? After all, the idea of an angel disguised as a tramp walking through the streets of Soho is just silly…isn't it? But why did he know about Johnny? *How* did he know about Johnny? And why does she know as a matter of absolute certainty that she *is* going to tell Johnny exactly what that dirty, rich, famous, abusive piece of filth did to her?

'Fakes, Freaks, Cheats Liars & Celebrities' *is available now as an ebook or paperback.*

Printed in Great Britain
by Amazon